T0158667

CAGES

CAGES

LOVE AND VENGEANCE IN A RED-LIGHT DISTRICT

AABID SURTI

Translated by Aalif Surti

PENGUIN
VIKING

An imprint of Penguin Random House

VIKING

USA | Canada | UK | Ireland | Australia
New Zealand | India | South Africa | China

Viking is part of the Penguin Random House group of companies
whose addresses can be found at global.penguinrandomhouse.com

Published by Penguin Random House India Pvt. Ltd
7th Floor, Infinity Tower C, DLF Cyber City,
Gurgaon 122 002, Haryana, India

Penguin
Random House
India

First published in Gujarati as *Vasaksajja* by Lokpriya Prakashan, Bombay, in 1979
Published in English in Viking Books by Penguin Random House India 2021

ISBN 9780670092703

Typeset in Adobe Garamond Pro by Manipal Technologies Limited, Manipal
Printed at Thomson Press India Ltd, New Delhi

www.penguin.co.in

Preface

'I am a prostitute by birth, by vocation, by religion. No man tricked me into this calling. No bastard deceived me. No pimp forced me into a cage. Unlike other innocent girls who are unwittingly trapped in the flesh trade, I have never shed a tear. I chose this ancient profession because it gives me complete satisfaction.'

These are the views of Kumud (name changed), the protagonist of this biographical work. From the dark alleys of Kamathipura, Bombay's red-light district, in the 1960s, she rose to become an actress who played the lead role in a Bollywood movie.

Originally written in Gujarati as *Vasaksajja*, the book has been translated into Hindi, Marathi, Urdu, Kannada, Bangla and English. In the 1980s, *Imprint*, one of India's most reputed literary magazines of the time, published an abridged, censored version of the book in two parts. Now the uncensored, expanded and updated version of the book is in your hands. Also, a fresh translation has been done for this special edition.

Before I conclude, I must express my thanks to Satish Purohit and Nikita Dudani for their attempts at drawing up a rough draft. A salute to my friend and editor, Dinesh Sinha of Byword Books (Delhi), for his efforts on polishing the draft. And finally, I am grateful to my son, Aalif, for helping me to prepare this fresh translation in English.

Aabid Surti
5 May 2020

1

Kumud.

Yes, that is my name. There is nothing special about it—and if there is any significance, I am not aware of it. I know only this: throughout my life, my name has often been disfigured (Cuckoo). It has been broken and reassembled (Kammu Jaan). Like some poet's nom de plume, my name has been conferred epithets (Kumud Kamathipura-waali). Many strange forms has my name taken (The Girl with the Golden Tooth).

Yet, I am Kumud. I have clung to my name the way a convict on death row clings to hope. But a condemned man's hope inevitably proves to be futile: in the end, he must give up his attachment to life and embrace the noose. So I feel that I too must shed all attachment with my name and accept reality.

Shakespeare had asked, 'What's in a name?' If someone calls a rose a radish, will it begin smelling putrid? No. But when Kumud is called Cuckoo or Kammu Jaan, she does not remain the same. With every new name, Kumud embodies a new persona. With every new title, she offers men a new fragrance. Today, once again, the time has come to discuss a new name for me.

Even though none of my old names were my choice, at least they had some connection with me. 'Cuckoo' was conferred upon me by a customer who was intoxicated by my sweet voice. One of my teeth has a gold cap that catches the sun when I smile. So it was not unexpected when someone nicknamed me 'The Girl with The Golden Tooth'. I began my career on the streets of Kamathipura, Bombay's red-light district, so I was called Kumud Kamathipura-waali.

But . . .

Today the list of names proposed has nothing to do with me. They are pretty names though. Beguiling. Syllables that conjure up visions of a fresh-faced, giggling girl untouched by the world.

Eventually, the choice has to be mine. What should my new name be? Pinky or Bobby? I have chosen these two favourites from a shortlist of ten. I like them both—they are trendy, modern names. But I cannot have both, of course. So, right now, my problem is which name I should choose to define the next phase of my life.

Bobby.

I settle upon this name—it feels tomboyish and fun. Sitting beside me is the producer of the film, Mr Ganguly. After a few moments of contemplation, he points out that some years ago there was a starlet called Bobby who had made her screen debut in a film called *Maikhana*. The film, and her career, sank that weekend. Instead of choosing the flop name of a flop actress in a flop film, why didn't I go for the fresher choice: Pinky?

The cinematographer, Mr Malhotra, and the scriptwriter, Aabid, both seated to my right, nod thoughtfully in agreement. I ponder over the matter for a few seconds and accept. From today, I will be called Pinky. My real name will disappear into the past, my new name will be painted on banners in city squares and on the walls of faraway villages.

Regulars from my past may wonder—is this Pinky the same old Kumud of Kamathipura? Maybe if they see my photograph, with my name, their doubts might be confirmed. Or they may still be fooled. After all, I am not that person any more. Like my name, I have left my history behind too.

And what, you may wonder, was this history? I'm sorry if it disappoints you to know that there is no glorious, uplifting message in my story. No moral lesson at the end. This is not the story of Sita, Savitri or the Blessed Virgin Mary. To those hoping for an inspirational tale of such noble and refined women, I would suggest that it will be wise to stop reading right now and get a refund for their hard-earned money. I do not want anyone who reads my story to curse me for my way of life, which I chose. Or, even worse, to pity me.

I declare, without guilt or hesitation, that I have led a life that is free—beyond that even, if there is anything. I am a prostitute by birth, by vocation and by religion. No man tricked me into this profession. No boyfriend dumped me here. No pimp forced me into these cages. Unlike the girls who sob every night because they were unwittingly entrapped in the flesh trade, I never shed a tear! On the contrary, I found that this ancient profession suited me. It made my soul content.

Playing the role of a god-fearing *pativrata biwi*—devoting my entire life to one man—I would have found neither contentment nor fortune. Or if I had been like the thousands of young women who work in offices, my days would have been a joyless routine and my nights would have neither adventure nor ecstasy. That kind of life never excited me. Amidst the seething sea of half-living bodies that crowd the sunless prisons you call offices, I would not even have realized where I had lost myself.

To such a dismal existence, I would much rather prefer suicide. I respect the ones you call fallen women more than upright housewives. Dig deep into the mind of any pativrata—that loyal slave married to a single man—and you will definitely find many men lying in dark corners. Peep into the heart of a whore who beds hundreds of men and you will be amazed to discover just one man sitting on the throne within.

My arguments, like me, may be too raw for your taste, but it's only because I show you the naked truth. Beyond that, it is up to you to unravel the answer to my first question: Which of these two women deserves to be placed on a pedestal?

I can understand if you are still struggling to make up your mind. I don't blame you. I blame the rotten corpse of a society you were brought up in. It's natural that its rancid stench would stick to you all your life.

I do, however, have one request: Try to keep the windows of your mind open. Some fresh air will certainly come in. Try to keep the doors to your heart open. Some morning breeze from the mountains in my village, which kisses flowers in the valleys, will refresh your body and soul. Science may have penetrated deep into the body, but who can fathom the mysteries of the soul?

I am reminded of the story of two best friends who were out for an evening walk. One of them suggested that they spend the evening at the *mujra*; the other insisted that it would be more fruitful to spend the evening listening to *hari-katha* at the temple. Both were obstinate—they could not come to an agreeable solution. So they went in opposite directions: one to the dancing girl's *kotha* and the other to participate in the kirtan.

Within an hour of listening to hari-katha, the devout one was nudged by pangs of boredom. His thoughts flew to his friend, imagining all the gaiety he was missing. If only he had listened to his friend and gone to the kotha, he would have been amidst dancing girls with kohl-lined eyes. He began fantasizing about their jiggling breasts and swinging hips, those lush, curvaceous bodies undulating to the *thap-thap-thap* of the tabla and the siren-call of the sarangi. How fast time would have passed!

At the kotha, the other friend's mind was on quite the opposite thing. He pictured his devout friend immersed in a soulful bhajan. How he wished he had listened to that idiot! He would sleep so peacefully tonight—and wake up fresh tomorrow, not hung-over and filled with self-loathing.

My beloved reader, here is my second question for you: Which of the two friends would you respect? The one whose body was in the temple but whose mind was in the kotha? Or the one who, even amidst the mesmerizing mujra, was yearning for the peace of God?

I ask you this because the difference between the so-called 'respectable' woman and the so-called 'fallen' woman is the same as the distance between these two friends. A distance each one of us has to cover during our own journeys.

Between Kumud and Pinky, too, there is a distance of many miles. I am Kumud, but I am Pinky too. Yet, I feel that today Pinky is not that Kumud. Neither was Kumud this Pinky. Pinky is an actress of tomorrow. Kumud was the whore of yesterday. In a way this difference, too, is not so significant.

I am a prostitute. I was a prostitute. I have always been a prostitute. Aai, my mother, was an unknown prostitute in Maharashtra's Satara district. We lived in a small village called Tulu. I was around seven years old when I began wondering about life, especially the truths that paraded before my eyes.

It was all strange and very confusing. There was a constable with a big, bushy moustache, whom I used to watch through a crack in the door. Every night, he would come home with a bottle of country liquor. He and Aai would spend hours drinking glass after glass of that fire-like water. It seemed to make them cheerful. They would giggle and occasionally laugh uproariously.

Then, when the bottle was empty, the constable would attempt to climb on top of Aai, as if she was a bolster. She would laugh and push him away with both hands. She would then turn up the flame of the kerosene lantern to hunt for a small packet of rubber balloons under the mattress, giggling as if someone was tickling her.

Then she would extinguish the lantern. On full-moon nights, the moonlight would filter in through the glass tile on the roof, lighting up Aai's room in an unearthly glow. I would see them hugging and bouncing. But on most nights the room would turn as black as the ink I used in school, and in that darkness, laughter would turn into loud breathing and then into a scream in which Aai always remembered Goddess Yellamma.

Maybe that was Aai's way of worshipping? I wasn't far from the truth in my innocent wonderings. From my bed, I loved watching the perfect blackness of moonless nights. For hours I would gaze at the black velvet sky caressing the diamond-like stars; sometimes I would foolishly attempt to count them and fall asleep before I could finish. God knows what I was searching for in those stars. Perhaps a dawn, a new hope?

I loved the first rays of the sun. Come morning, I would hoist the bundle of washing on to my head and skip along like a happy heifer to the river. The village folk would be goggle-eyed. Something about my walk made them so glad that everyone, from small shopkeepers to big moneylenders, would stop to look as I walked past.

If you count in years, I was still an unripe mango. But looking at my body, nobody could have guessed that. At the age of thirteen, I could easily pass off for a curvy sixteen-year-old. Perhaps the warmth from the stares of the men in the village had heated my body, forcing it to ripen before it was time!

While I was attractive—at least to men—I never considered myself beautiful. I was neither fair nor dark-skinned—my skin was the colour of honey. My features, too, were ordinary, like that of a normal village girl. However, there was something unique about me that set me apart from the other girls.

Maybe that uniqueness was the fire burning within me—the lightning flowing through my veins. Whatever the reason, the way men looked at me was different, and that reminded me that I was not just another village girl.

By my sixteenth birthday, I had become aware of quite a few secrets about the female body—even though no man had touched me yet. Whatever knowledge I had gathered was from observing Aai. She was an experienced prostitute who knew the rare art of taming men. How to flatter men, how to clean their pockets and yet maintain a hold over them—from her I learnt all the tricks of the trade.

One secret though I could not unlock. Every man she slept with believed that he was her one true love and the rest were just clients. Every man used to boast about this confidently. Even today, I have the highest respect for Aai. One reason for this is because she knew how to tame men.

Despite welcoming innumerable men into her body, she allowed only one man to enter her heart. Constable Naik. I don't recall her ever trying to make money off him. On the contrary, I observed that it was he who often took small loans from her.

Aai never refused him. She knew Constable Naik was the father of four kids. His heart was pure. He never accepted bribes. To provide for a family with honest police wages was close to impossible, so she sometimes helped him tide over tight situations.

After the birth of his second child, Constable Naik sought refuge in the bottle. With the cost of buying a bottle every day, over and above the expenses of running a house, his miserable life went from bad to worse. He began to shamelessly ask for money every other day.

One day, my mother tried to reason with him. 'Look, Naik, you can't go on like this! Last year, our village had a poor harvest. The prices of vegetables and pulses are shooting up. If it does not rain this year—'

Then? This question nailed itself on his forehead. This one question carried the weight of a hundred questions, one he appeared to crumble beneath. The answer was unthinkable: Daily necessities would soar above the grasp of the poor. Fistfuls of currency notes would not buy a handful of grains. Moreover, he had already been warned by the department thrice: If he did not quit drinking, he would be sacked. And if that happened—?

Then? This second question lodged itself even deeper inside Constable Naik, like a bullet in his chest. Aai begged him again to give up the bottle. But a brain soggy with alcohol loses its capacity to reason—what went in through one of Constable Naik's ear spilled out through the other.

Aai's predictions proved prophetic. Constable Naik was suspended. Drought set in. Days of hunger test even the toughest man's mettle. And Constable Naik—Aai's pure-hearted, beloved Naik who was as innocent as a child—could not endure it. Hunger drove him insane and he took his own life.

In that savage drought, Aai's love story ended and my journey began.

The deadly famine drove men to desperate lengths to fill their bellies; they lost their appetite for sex. Aai's trade slumped. As it was, she had lost interest in life after Constable Naik's death. All day, she remained morose. She would stare at the wall, hoping that it would turn into a cinema screen playing happy memories of the nights she spent with Constable Naik under the glow of the moonlight seeping in from the translucent glass.

Sometimes, in the dead of the night, she would sit up startled and, like the widow of a noble family, shed silent tears. At times, I would find her feeling wretched and weeping unbearably. I would try to calm her down, but she would look at me blankly and then turn her eyes to the open sky beyond the window.

The cloudless sky had nothing to offer to us—neither hope nor joy, neither a morsel of food nor a sip of water. The river that ran through our village had long gone dry. Those who could afford it were abandoning the village. I tried to explain to Aai that no one would survive for long in that inhospitable ghost town.

This news alarmed her—her eyes scanned me from head to toe. Due to the famine, my body wasn't filled out like before. The lightning had stopped running in my veins and even the spark in my eyes was rapidly dying out.

I held her hands and told her, 'The village will be deserted before the month ends, Aai.' She was still silent. 'It will be difficult to even breathe in these ruins.'

Aai's dead eyes began to flicker back to life. As if she had not heard a single word, she asked, 'What are you trying to say?'

'We should go to Bombay, Aai.'

Once again, she sank into her own thoughts. She was attached to the scrubby soil of Tulu. The water of this land was like the blood running through her body. She was born here and wanted to return to the red soil with the flames.

After communicating this—her final wish—to me, she arranged for me to move to Bombay with a family from our neighbourhood. We trusted the Pandurangas implicitly. Our relationship with them was time-tested. Yet, I was unwilling to leave Aai behind to die all alone.

Aai patiently persuaded me all night. Suppressing her suffering, she made an effort to help me see the situation clearly. She pleaded with me to accept reality. 'Kumud, even if the drought had not struck this year, I would have sent you to Bombay. There is neither a present nor a future for prostitutes in this little village. What is the population of Tulu anyway? A little over three thousand? Among these, how many are men? And among them, how many are rich? And amongst the rich men, how many have a taste for the pleasures of the flesh?'

I looked at her, stunned. With mathematical precision she had laid out my future business prospects in Tulu. What she had said was true—a prostitute had no scope in this dusty village. After so many decades in the business, people still called Aai a '*do damdi ki raand*', a two-penny whore.

Aai was persistent about me migrating to Bombay because of what had happened to our village potter, Waghmare. In a matter of just a few years, his run-down shanty on the outskirts had turned into a pukka house roofed with fancy tiles. His son's new motorcycle was always parked in the verandah, near the cowshed. Although he didn't have a refrigerator, a dead TV set proudly stood in the sitting room waiting for the promised power supply. The set was housed in a wooden cabinet facing the main entrance so that no passer-by would miss it.

The secret of Waghmare's prosperity was not his fertile land but his fertile wife who, in just four years, had delivered five girls, including a set of twins. That was two decades ago. Today, three of his girls were working in an upper-class brothel on Shuklaji Street, right in the heart of Kamathipura. The fourth one had become a call girl in Juhu, and the fifth one, who had just turned fifteen, was set to board the train to Bombay the following year.

We, on the other hand, were living off Aai's income in Tulu, were still dirt poor—beggars without begging bowls.

I thought over my decision that night. The metropolis had captured my fantasy. Visions of tall towers kissing the sky, which I had only seen in magazines and movies until then, began floating before my eyes. A few years ago, two other girls from our village—curly-haired Champa and bright-eyed Hema—had gone to Bombay. When they returned after a year to celebrate Ganesh Chaturthi, so much gold sparkled off their bodies that it blinded us. My mother's wrists, even today, are as bare as a widow's.

With every passing hour, I was more convinced—the city of gold was for me. I was born for it. It was my destiny. But I did not want to leave Aai behind to suffer alone.

The following morning, the Panduranga family also joined the exodus—leaving behind an empty house and acres of parched farmland. Most families around them had already left. The few that remained in our mohalla were planning their departure.

The population of Tulu had dipped to one-third. Humanity had fallen much lower. Rotting bodies of both human beings and animals lay strewn on the scorched earth. Crows and vultures descended to fight over the carcasses. A searing wind blew unceasingly across the cracked land.

Amidst this apocalyptic atmosphere, as if from nowhere, a truck appeared in the village, raising hope and dust in its wake. I was with Aai at the time, foraging for edible roots and tubers in some long-dried bushes.

Her eyes turned in the direction of the truck and her weary face lit up with a smile. You might think an angel had descended from heaven, the way she started running towards it. She held on to my wrist tightly as I stumbled along, trying to keep up with her.

I still could not understand whose truck this was. What was it doing in our godforsaken village? It didn't seem to be carrying any consignment either.

The truck stopped under a barren banyan tree. The driver and cleaner were standing outside, resting against the bonnet, and puffing beedis. The driver, a Jat, gave me a quick once-over before addressing Aai in surprise.

'Lakshmi Bai, you are still alive!'

'This is my daughter,' she mustered a reply.

His name was Bhajan Lal. Once again, this time more deliberately, he inspected my shrivelled body from head to toe as he took a long drag of his beedi. I looked down at my feet, self-conscious. The blistering heat was making snakes of sweat crawl down my bony back. Meanwhile, three more women had rushed to the spot with their young daughters. Bhajan Lal inhaled and exhaled leisurely, sizing up the girls with every drag.

In a few minutes, the crowd had swelled. There were some men in the crowd too. They, too, had brought their daughters along. A slave market had sprung up. Girls from ten to twenty-five years of age were standing before him, all available at throwaway prices. Taking one last drag, Bhajan Lal began to choose. He pointed to the girls who still had some flesh on their bodies. He selected about ten. I stood a few feet away with Aai.

Aai could not bear it. She began howling. She fell at Bhajan Lal's feet, pleading that he take me along, begging him to show some mercy. This absurd drama was being played out under the white-hot afternoon sun and gusts of burning wind.

'Lakshmi Bai!' Bhajan Lal said gruffly, swatting Aai away like a fly. 'Your daughter is a bundle of bones, and I don't trade in bones.'

What Bhajan Lal had said was true; he was a trader of flesh. Once a year, he would bring his truck to our village, buy girls for Rs 200–300 each and return to Bombay. There he would get Rs 500–1000 for a girl, sometimes more. It was understandable. He would not throw money on a skeleton.

Aai, however, continued grovelling. 'I am not asking you for Rs 200 . . . give me anything! I will accept it as prasad from the temple.'

Bhajan Lal was shrewd. He knew the families were desperate. Instead of Rs 200, girls were going for as less as Rs 50. In the end, he placed a ten-rupee note in Aai's hand and, in the blink of an eye, I was sold! I could feel tears welling up.

Aai put her hand on my head. 'Don't cry, my child. At least one of us will have a chance at survival now. Once you begin earning in Bombay, you can help me too. Thanks to you, I might live after all.'

I began to sob like never before—the sorrow of parting mixed with tears of hope. But they were not the fearful sobs of the scared girls around me. They were tears of a *dulhan* leaving her *maika*, a bride leaving her home.

2

Would you be surprised if I told you that in the early days my rate was just two rupees? I was doing business in the lanes of Kamathipura. Any man who placed two shiny one-rupee coins in my palm could buy me for a shot.

I had no roof over my head. Nor was there place for me in any cage. Bhajan Lal, the truck driver who thought he had conned Aai when he bought me for ten rupees, soon regretted his decision. All the other girls who had come with me in that truck had been sold by now.

Some were picked up for the cages, while others found a place in numbered bungalows. Some girls earned him Rs 500, others Rs 800 and even more. I was the only unfortunate one whom the dalals, or the brokers, and madams of the red-light district were not interested in deflowering.

Bhajan Lal did not give up. He hoped some Marwari shopkeeper would buy me for Rs 50. As a side business, shopkeepers in Kamathipura sometimes bought the girls no kotha wanted and worked them—at the end of the night they would grab a portion of the girl's earnings, with a topping of interest.

Like a goat being led to the abattoir, Bhajan Lal took me to a Marwari's shop. The portly Marwari did not even bother to look at me. Instead, for half an hour, he kept arguing with a customer. The customer, a *tapori*, or a vagabond, wanted to sell him the shiny polyester-blended Terylene shirt he was wearing. They were haggling over the price. The Marwari's argument was that it was no doubt a new shirt, but it was cheap cotton terrycot. The tapori was furiously insisting that it was pure, expensive Terylene.

Finally, after much haggling, they agreed on a deal for Rs 7.50. The customer took off his shirt right there and threw it on the counter. The Marwari counted seven notes of one rupee each and a fifty-paisa coin. The man marched out of the shop, shirtless.

Now the Marwari looked up at us.

'Tekchand!' Bhajan Lal said with hollow enthusiasm, pointing at me. 'I picked up this item especially for you from Satara.'

The Marwari turned his dead-fish eyes towards me. From his gaze, it was obvious that I was worth as much as a tyre, a clock or a terrycot shirt for him. Perhaps even less. A single sweeping glance was enough for his experienced eyes.

'What will I do with this shrivelled plant?' he said flatly to Bhajan Lal. 'Take her away.'

Bhajan Lal did not budge.

'Go, go! Get lost, man! Trying to fool me with this dried twig . . .'

'Tekchand, sprinkle a few drops and this dried twig will bloom again.'

'*You* water it,' the Marwari said dryly. 'When she blooms, bring her back.'

'Tekchand, you're getting her for nothing.'

'I don't want her.'

'Just fifty rupees . . .?'

'No one is going to give you fifty paisa for this girl,' he said with resounding finality.

Bhajan Lal accepted defeat. He left me to my fate. For a few moments, even I felt bad for myself but then I steeled myself. Self-pity was a luxury I could not afford. I thought of Aai, slowly starving to death in the village. Her fate line had been as weak as the man she had loved. I was her last hope. I shrugged away my tears and considered my situation. What could I do? Where could I go? At least I was in Bombay, in Kamathipura, the carnal capital of the country's sex trade.

No one could stop me from working on the streets. So I decided to begin there. I tried my luck in crowded places like bus stops, near restaurants, outside cinema houses—wherever men congregated. I was ready to work under parked trucks with oil dripping, in dark alleys with the stench of sewers, and in abandoned buildings with swarms of mosquitoes.

I found solace only in knowing that there were other girls like me who had no place to call home. They would go out in groups to solicit clients on the streets. I joined one such gang. Like a school of fish, we would move around all night. Before dawn, we would look for a clean spot on the footpath to sleep. We would wake up when the sun was overhead to have our breakfast—watery sambar with stale pav—at a roadside tea stall.

Dinner was rarely a problem. Someone would always prefer our company to eating alone. But mostly, he would uncork a bottle of Musambi, cheap country liquor, before dinner and would expect us to keep him company in that too.

Just one peg. Refuse and we would go without food.

This was one of the reasons why many girls were addicted to liquor. Somehow, I had managed to keep away from alcohol. Whenever I saw a liquor bottle, Aai's face would float before my eyes—begging Constable Naik to stop consuming the poison before it consumed him. With that, I would be reminded once again that I had left her alone, amidst a severe drought. My worry for her was a constant thorn in my side.

Did she have anything to eat? Was she still scrabbling at the dry earth for roots? Or had her body given up?

I was helpless. I was not in a position to do anything for her yet. In fact, each day I too was on the brink of starvation. Apart from my emaciated frame that put men off, I was not street-smart. Most men chose my friends over me. It was frustrating. I began trying even harder.

After sunset, I would mingle with the gang of girls I was familiar with and we would fan out around the ticket window of Alfred Talkies, an old, pre-Independence cinema built by the British. There, in the crowded Falkland Road neighbourhood, the evenings would become livelier as the night would advance. Under the light of the street lamps, working-class men with paan in their mouths and desire in their eyes would pass me by. While the other girls would confidently snatch men like eagles pick out fish from the water, I would stand rooted, studying their faces—like a person without a ticket standing anxiously at the cinema gate, searching for his elusive 'extra' ticket in the passing faces.

Within a few days, I learnt how to read from afar the lust in a man's eyes. Stealthily, I would begin moving towards him. But before I could claim my prey, the other wild cats would pounce on him. A free-for-all would break out.

A first-timer in Kamathipura would be terrified by such an unexpected assault of powdered women with harsh voices. But if he was a seasoned veteran, with a few stinging slaps, he would whack the whores aside. Then he would pick the girl of his choice and walk off with a cocky swagger.

I had been slapped more than ten times in the past few days and no longer had the courage to participate in the savage trial of strength. I felt helpless. There was no place for sensitivity or charm in that lawless jungle. Neither was there anybody I could confide in.

Occasionally, when I came across a girl from my village, I would chat with her. Chandra and I had grown up in the same mohalla. She, too, had come to Bombay with me. Fate had been kinder to her though. She had found a place in a cage. Every evening, she would step out to buy paan at the street corner. She would proceed to stuff two Banarasi paans at a time into her mouth, gossip with me and then buy some more for the night.

In those few minutes, we would chat freely, emboldened by our memories. Mostly it was she who talked—about the childhood days of freedom and innocence—and I who listened, fascinated. Her lips would shine red from the betel juice, brighter and more glamorous than any lipstick. Then, having conferred the privilege of her time and memories upon me, she would leave for her cage, her hips swaying provocatively.

I felt envious when she spoke of her life in the cage. She had everything that I dreamt of—four solid walls with a roof above, a cot with a mattress below and a door fitted with iron rods.

However, Chandra had something more. She had regular clients. Had Goddess Yellamma appeared before me in those days to grant me a wish, I would have said, 'My ultimate wish is to find a place in a cage.'

The uncertainty of life on the street was taking a toll on me. On some nights, all I did was hunt till morning for a client while the other girls who worked on the same lanes managed to hook at least a dozen with their wholesome bodies. I had no such luck.

On one such night, I looked down at my bony physique. My collarbones jutted out like coat hangers. If I could barely manage to find two-rupee customers, how would I find a man who loved me, with whom I could share all joys and sorrows at the end of a long, dark night?

Depression began to haunt me. I desperately missed home. I looked up. The night sky was blotted with smutty phosphorescent lights. I remembered the ink-black sky of Tulu sparkling with diamond stars. The stars were calling out to me—come back, sweet angel!

My eyes turned moist. Most of all, I was missing Aai. I wished I could lie down with my head in her lap so she could smooth the frown on my forehead with her caresses. But even before a tear could trickle down my cheek, I would wipe it off. I would remind myself that neither was crying a solution, nor was losing hope. I had to find a way out. I had entered this profession of my own free will, and it was up to me to take it ahead now. Every business faces teething troubles, I told myself. I had to work with my limitations and find solutions.

As I looked deeper into my problem, it dawned on me that while most girls accosted clients under the streetlights, a few solicited in the dark corners. Why didn't all girls work under the lights? I had no answers yet.

To find out, I entered a dark alley in Kamathipura. As I walked, I tried to discern the girls' faces, but all I could see were shifting shadows. I could guess that those shadows, too, were looking at me. But obviously, no one could see me clearly.

Within a few moments, this illusion was broken. A girl's voice called out my name softly. Surprised, I peered into the darkness and saw a shadow moving towards me.

Who was this girl?

She approached me and I stared at the features that emerged from the gloom. But as the face became clear, I saw that it was not a face—only a shadow of what someone's face had once been.

'Forgot me so soon?' The voice had a familiar ring to it. 'Kumud, I am Champa.'

'Oh, it's you!' I could not believe my ears. Or my eyes for that matter.

Champa had been my best friend as a child. We were born in the same village and studied in the same school, under the same banyan tree, till the fourth standard. We used to walk hand in hand on the banks of the river that wound through our village.

I remember more, but none of that matters now. When Champa was eleven, Bhajan Lal's truck came to the village for the first time. A few hours later, the truck left for Bombay, taking Champa and a few other girls, leaving a dust storm behind.

At that time, I had no idea that my eleven-year-old playmate was going to the big city to sell her virginity to the highest bidder. I wasn't even old enough then to grasp the idea of someone negotiating the price for a bud that had not blossomed yet. If I recall correctly, I was three years younger than Champa; I was twenty when I met her in the dark alley that night, which would make Champa twenty-three.

When she was sixteen, Champa had returned to our village from Bombay for the first time. I had run across the village to meet her with so much excitement! I remember how she had glittered! Ten gold bangles on each hand, a heavy gold necklace with a deep red stone resting on her cleavage, gold leaves dangling from her ears. (Aai later told me that it was imitation gold. The ruby, too, was no precious stone. 'All things that are white are not milk, and all that glitters is not gold,' she always reminded me.)

Even though her body was not yet fully formed, it had seemed like Champa had stepped into womanhood. Her sixteen-year-old body had appeared to have seen twenty summers. Ignoring the mystified look on my face, she had filled my ears with magical stories. Bombay, she had told me, was the city of gold.

'Loot as much as you can with both hands, still its treasures overflow,' she had said and then gently added, 'Kumud, your

Aai has wasted her life in this dust bowl. Don't make the same mistake. If she had pursued her trade in Bombay, today, in place of the crumbling ruins you call home, there would have been a grand haveli.'

Imagining the magnificent mansion, my eyes had lit up with rainbows. I had run home to ask Aai this question: Aai, why didn't you go to Bombay? But Aai had been fast asleep with her beloved Constable Naik. If there was one person responsible for our sorry state, it was that Constable Naik! Aai had loved him with all her heart. And she had loved him for many years. Even after he had got married she had not forgotten him. Why her whole world collapsed when Naik committed suicide was not hard to understand.

I caught hold of Champa's wrist and pulled her out of the dark lane. As the stark light of the street lamp hit her face, my breath stopped. Was I hallucinating? Before me was an old lady of twenty-three! And she was saying her name was Champa! The same Champa who had been my childhood friend!

With eyes as wide as saucers, I kept staring at Champa. Countless wrinkles, like an infestation of worms, crawled across her face. Her blood-red eyes had sunk deep into their sockets below which jutted out fleshless cheekbones. Her hair had fallen out and a dirty scarf covered her bald head. Her body looked like a decayed tree stump.

'What are you looking at?' she asked with a pale smile.

'I am looking for my sweet childhood friend, Champa.'

'Or perhaps you are looking at your own future?'

Jolted, I let go of her wrist. The question travelled down my body like a lead weight, making me sink with it. Champa was not far off the mark. It was inevitable that my time, too, would come to an end someday. But I had never imagined that the end could be as horrifying as the one facing me. A shiver ran down my spine.

I changed the topic. 'What were you doing there in that dark corner?'

'Who will come near me if I stand in the light? Darkness protects me, conceals my identity. When a stray drunkard or junkie staggers into this lane, I earn a couple of rupees . . . enough to survive on pav and chai.'

The mystery of the dark alley had been revealed to me. How ugly the faces, how shrivelled the bodies of the women who shunned the bright circles under the street lights must be! Yet they had to live because they did not have the courage to take their lives.

Champa and I exchanged memories of happier times. Once again, I remembered the day sixteen-year-old Champa had come back to the village and confided in me with sparkling eyes: Bombay is the city of gold! Loot as much as you can with both hands, still its treasures overflow. Reality looked so different. This city of gold had looted Champa—it had squeezed her dry, crushed her and then discarded her. Whose fault was it?

I thought about it long and hard. Had Champa taken care of her body right from the start, she would perhaps not have been in such a mess. Blinded by the flash of gold, Champa seemed to have forgotten that a woman's body was only flesh and bones—not a machine. And even a machine has its limits. If it is worked night and day without a break, it will fall apart before its time.

Champa had also fallen apart before her time. Her body had become a factory that manufactured diseases. Any man who had sex with her got a parting gift of one or two infections. The man, in turn, shared it with his wife. After all, hadn't the man vowed to share everything with his wife, for better or worse, in sickness and health, till death do them part?

3

When someone calls me by my new name—Pinky—it makes me giggle. For a moment I forget that I am not really Pinky; I am Kumud. Sometimes I ask myself—am I really Kumud?

And then reality falls around me again like a net. I frantically pull at the cords of my traumatic past to escape, but I cannot extricate myself. The moment I am alone in a quiet corner, all those nights and days start closing in on me once again.

At times, I feel terribly alone even in a crowd. From the present, I wander away. Faraway. Back into the netherworld where shadows beckon to lost men. Back to the street corners smelling of sweat, semen and sour alcohol. Back to the hellish nights when starvation awaited me at sunrise. Then I remember Champa who taught me how to use the cover of darkness to trap men, and I feel grateful.

My income increased though I had to drop my rate by half—even drunk men were not willing to pay more than a rupee to the faceless girls who worked in the pitch-black bylanes. Our vaginas were nothing more than cheap complaint boxes for the failures and frustrations that alcohol wasn't able to drown. For me, it was enough that I was getting customers. If nothing else, at least I was earning enough to have two square meals.

There was a special arrangement made to entertain clients in the back alleys—a washed-up old whore had ingeniously put together a bug-free shack for prostitutes. Nothing more than a charpoy and a bucket of water with a tumbler. For every client we brought, we gave her fifty-paisa commission.

My shrivelled body began to blossom again. Flesh began to smoothen out around my jutting ribs. My hips regained their curves and my breasts began to swell. A glint of life reappeared in my eyes as delicious contours covered my bony body.

'Kumud,' Champa said during one of our evening walks, 'you don't need the purdah of darkness any more. Go back under the lamps. You will easily find two-rupee clients.'

'No, Champa! I like your company, I want to stay—'

'It's best for your future if you step into the light.'

'Champa, if I ever leave this place, it will be for a cage.'

We were strolling along the footpath on Falkland Road, which was lined with cages. I could feel my heart throbbing as I observed the girls standing by the doors. Some of them sat on the verandahs in short skirts, offering the open invitation of their thighs. Others stood chewing on paans in sexy cholis that barely contained the fullness of their chests. While most of them were blowing kisses and enticing passers-by with lewd signs, some of the dusky south Indian girls were tempting men by suggestively jiggling their voluptuous bodies. Whether sitting or standing, every girl had her own peculiar style. For example, one girl standing in a cage near the corner of Kolsa Gali created a seductive triangle between her thighs by putting one foot over the knee of her other leg.

There was a hustle-bustle of clients in front of every cage door. Men were bargaining like customers in a fish market, deals were being struck with a smooch. The air was alive with laughter and the tinkling of bangles. The girls' powdered faces were painted with rouge, their eyes were lined with kajal and their red lips were spreading smiles everywhere. A constable was swinging his baton as he took a leisurely round. I remembered Chandra who was ensconced in one of these cages and felt a twinge of envy.

Daylight was fading. It was *dhanda* time. Champa was getting restless, but I was not in the mood to work that night. I had earned double yesterday so I could afford to take one night off.

I shared a spontaneous idea with her. 'How about watching a movie tonight?'

Champa neither accepted nor declined my offer. Over the last ten days, I had taken on responsibility for her. If she didn't make any money on a night, I would share two rupees from my earnings with her so that she did not have to sleep hungry. She was grateful.

From Falkland Road, we sauntered up to Taj Theatre. The movie *Revolver Rani* had released two days ago. Whenever my eyes would fall on the giant film marquee, I would stare at it and admire how powerful the heroine was—sitting on horseback, revolver in hand, as if she would pull the trigger and some evil man would fall by the wayside.

Her rosy-cheeked beauty would bring to my mind the painted girls who adorned the cages. I always wondered when I would get a chance to stand proudly in a cage. I was doubtful if that would ever happen for me. All the same, I decided that if fate did land me in a cage someday, I would dress like Revolver Rani. Blue jeans, dark jacket and revolver in hand—that would be my trademark. If any man tried to haggle or act tough, I would shoot the bastard point-blank.

As I entered the theatre with Champa, my eyes fell on a familiar face. For a few moments we stared at each other. Then he approached us. Champa recognized him too. Like me, she too had been brought to Bombay in his truck. But the Jat truck driver, Bhajan Lal, stared fixedly only at me, as if he didn't want to acknowledge Champa's existence.

'Wow!' His lips parted in amazement. 'What a delicious tandoori chicken you have turned into . . . that too in just three months.' He pinched my cheek.

Brushing aside his hand, I corrected him. 'Three and a half.'

He ignored my comment. 'When I brought you here, no *bhadwa* was ready to buy you for even ten rupees. But I don't regret it because I have been proven right. I told that Marwari Tekchand, "Water this plant and it will bloom," but nothing could penetrate that *chutiya*'s brain.'

The film began. The Jat took his seat. I knew he would return during the interval, and he did. As soon as the lights were turned on, I found him standing in the aisle next to my seat.

'Will you have tea?' he asked.

I declined.

'Come now . . .' he said, yanking at my wrist. 'I will treat you to pista kulfi.'

I pulled my arm free from his grip and glared at him. Respectable people and families sitting around us had turned with curious glances. Bhajan Lal hesitated. He had thought he would be able to have his way with me, as he did with the other street-walkers of Kamathipura. But he had forgotten one thing. I was not on the streets now. I was in a theatre watching a movie, just like the others. Fortunately, the lights began to dim again as the interval ended. Advertisement slides flickered on the screen. He stomped back to his seat, eyes bloodshot. I did not care.

The film was so gripping that I forgot everything else. The heroine's fiery and fearless fights . . . galloping to avenge the death of her brother . . . leaping from one hill to another on horseback . . . it was all so inspiring. Even girls like Champa, who had given up on life, found the courage to fight another day. As the movie ended, we headed for the exit.

'Bhajan Lal will be waiting outside,' I warned Champa.

'What do you intend to do?'

'That depends on what he intends to do.'

Huddled amidst the exiting crowd, we slowly made our way out. When we crossed the main gate, I was surprised. Bhajan Lal was nowhere to be seen. I scanned every corner of the street.

'Maybe he gave up and left,' Champa said.

We proceeded to have dinner at an Irani restaurant. With neat little Banarasi paans stuffed in our mouths, we parted ways. Champa left for the dark alley in search of customers while I stayed back—I had taken the night off, after all. I found a vacant verandah outside a closed shop to stretch my legs. But these were usually my working hours and sleep eluded me.

My thoughts carried me back to my village. Aai's face, stained with tears, flashed before my eyes. I had left her all alone to survive the drought. God knew if she was still breathing! One needs luck to survive calamities, and I knew Aai's palm had only one line—the line of bad luck.

But how wise was it to trust the folds of one's skin? One of Aai's customers, a stammering astrologer, used to say the line of fortune ran deep and wide across my palm, 'like the river K-k-Krishna'. Aai used to laugh and say that the way he said it meant it was three times as deep and wide.

But look at me now. I was sleeping on a grocer's verandah, with rats and pye-dogs for company. There was no roof above my head, no walls to protect me. Even a bathroom was a luxury. I would usually use a municipal tap to take a bath, that too during the darkest hour of the night. I would unwrap my wet sari and wear another one under the cover of darkness. Apart from a spare change of clothes, I owned nothing. In the morning, I would use the municipal lavatory to answer the call of nature. My life revolved around public utilities, public toilets and public taps.

My income was not sufficient to send a money order back home every month. Even though I sincerely wished I could save a rupee a day—to send Aai around thirty rupees each month for her basic needs—it was just not possible yet.

I do not know when I fell asleep. But I do remember dreaming of stars. Each star was the smiling face of a neighbour from the village. Aai's place was in a special star that had a golden aura.

Was she dead?

When my eyes opened, the sun was shining and Champa was looking at me, smiling gently. Perhaps she had nudged me awake. I stretched out with a long yawn before sitting up.

'Enjoyed your holiday sleep?' she asked playfully.

'What about you? Did you sleep or not?'

She shook her head and then added with a dramatic flourish, 'Now I will sleep in peace only after I help you reach the glorious heights where you belong.'

Standing up, I stretched drowsily again, only to realize mid-yawn that Champa had said something out of the ordinary. 'What did you say?'

'Quick! Get ready!' She laughed. 'I'll tell you everything in detail.'

'But what is it?'

She stood as silent as a temple idol.

At the public tap, I brushed my teeth and splashed some water on my face. After scrubbing off the last vestiges of sleep, I returned.

'Comb your hair properly.'

Her command was puzzling. Something was definitely afoot.

'Is it a rich customer?' I asked.

'What fool will wander in at this time of the day?'

'Then?'

Fixing my hairpins for me, she asked me to follow her, but I refused to budge.

'Look here, Champa! Until you tell me exactly what's happening, I'm not moving an inch. What's the big secret?'

She chuckled and then added, 'Your one and only wish in life is about to be fulfilled.'

I thought it over. My one and only wish was to find a place in a cage. Champa knew that. I looked at her wide-eyed as she grinned broadly in confirmation.

Still unable to believe Champa, I started walking quickly to keep up with her. Could she actually get me into a cage? When we arrived at the turning of the second lane of Kamathipura, she stopped in front of a house. I waited outside while she disappeared into the iron-barred doorway.

The tender rays of the morning sun were caressing my body. I was amazed to see my healthy curves in the shadow I cast—I could only imagine how filled out my face must be! It had been a month since I had seen myself in a mirror. Once in a while I would sneak a look at the decorated mirrors in the paan-beedi shop, but I had not seen my full reflection in a while. Where would those who do not own a house find a mirror?

When Champa emerged, she was accompanied by a stocky woman with a shrewd, pockmarked face who wore a very tight choli and a colourful nine-yard sari. She could easily have passed off for a middle-aged Maharashtrian housewife from the ghats. But her back was erect and her flattened silver hair was shining in the morning sunlight. On her nose rested silver-rimmed glasses precariously held together with knots of string.

She studied me from behind her glasses with interest, her experienced eyes unashamedly measuring every curve of my body. I stood quietly, eyes downcast. But inside, I had the same knot in my stomach that I got in school while waiting for my final examination results.

Moments later, the results were out. The woman smiled. I threw my arms around Champa and hugged her tightly, tears welling up in my eyes. 'Champa!' I exclaimed, as I stepped back, 'I will never forget what you have done for me.'

She left quietly.

Kumud Kamathipura-waali. I had been tagged with this identity ever since I had come to Bombay. But when I entered the cage my identity changed again—Kumud Pinjre-waali. I had finally found a place in a cage. With my trademark red lips and a touch of talc on my glowing face, I stood in style, holding the iron bars and showering generous smiles upon the men who passed by.

The sun had just set. The girls appeared like stars and stood in clusters, all lit up. The throng of men was thickening. In truth, it was only after sunset that this place began throbbing with the drumbeat of life. By dawn, the whole area turned flaccid again. The day would be spent lazing and yawning in bed. Compared to the night, I felt that the daylight hours passed excruciatingly slowly, like a wounded snake crawling.

Our madam, Sakhu Bai, was a caring soul. She addressed us girls as 'beti' and pampered us as if we actually were her daughters. Apart from me, there were three other girls—two giggly twins, Seethe-Geethe from south India; and Nirmala, a busty girl with black lipstick, from Pune. They welcomed me into their little circle of sisterhood.

My income, too, increased after entering the cage. From two rupees, my rate shot up to seven, of which Sakhu Bai kept half as commission. Servicing fifteen clients every night was not troublesome for me. However, I made sure not to sleep with more than ten men in a night.

'Why?' Nirmala, the buxom one, asked me one day.

'My wish,' I responded with a mysterious smile. She never asked again, but Sakhu Bai was unable to contain her curiosity—and there was a valid reason for that.

The clients I turned away would sometimes not choose any other girl and leave disheartened. That meant a hole in Sakhu Bai's profit. Her distress was natural; no madam in Kamathipura would allow this. The next time I turned clients away with a smile, she fought with me. I did not say a single word in my defence.

A few days passed. Late one night, I was standing holding the bars, waiting for my last client, when I saw a young boy glancing at me surreptitiously. I could tell that this was his first visit to a red-light district. He could not even muster the courage to look at my face.

I gazed at him with a twinkle in my eyes. When he finally looked up, I slipped my fingers into my blouse and teasingly pulled out an embroidered handkerchief, moving it around my face like a hand-held fan. His eyes were now locked on me. Slowly, he took tentative steps towards my cage. I came out of the cage and grabbed his wrist. The fish was trapped.

The inside of the cage was cramped. Like a joint family living in a *kholi*, we had adjusted to life in this tightly confined space. For furniture, there were just two beds, both surrounded by curtains, like mosquito nets, to give the customers a flimsy version of privacy.

Besides the beds, there was barely any space to sit or stand, except for a small corridor that allowed a single client to sidle up to the bed. Outside the cage, on the pavement, was a wooden stool, reserved for Sakhu Bai to sit on.

I led the boy into the cage. He sat gingerly on one corner of the bed. I noticed beads of perspiration gathering on his forehead. On the next bed, black-lipped Nirmala was having boisterous fun with a regular client. They were laughing bawdily, like donkeys braying. The sound of their laughter was so loud and clear that it felt as if it were our own. In this surreal atmosphere, the poor boy got even more fidgety.

I dabbed his face with my handkerchief. Amidst the floating curtains, he sat without a word in our private little world. He simply looked around bewildered, as if he had realized that a magician had locked him inside a trunk.

Suddenly, the curtain lifted and Sakhu Bai's pockmarked face peeped in. He jumped in fright. With a smile on my lips, I calmly explained to him that he had not paid yet. One by one, he fished out ten crumpled one-rupee notes. I gave seven rupees to Sakhu Bai and returned the rest to him. She left and the bedsheet-curtains fell around us once again.

The boy appeared more settled now, but he was yet to undo even a single button of his shirt or trousers. I helped him. I undid the buttons one by one and eased his shirt off. He took off his trousers on his own. Maybe he wanted to prove that he was a macho *mard*—and that he was ready to perform like one.

However, even before the performance began, I knew from experience that the curtain would not rise! And that is exactly what happened. I tried every trick in my book, but all my caresses, fondling and sweet-talking could not ignite any passion in his limp penis.

With time ticking, he began to plunge into despair. His manhood had betrayed him. He looked at me with wide eyes, full of questions. I wiped the sweat off his face once again and asked, 'What's your name?'

'Sadoba.'

'It happens . . . the first time, it can happen to any man. Even great wrestlers lose their first round when they enter this ring. You have no reason to feel ashamed. I'm certain that when you come again you will enjoy every drop of my love.'

Hearing my words, Sadoba's face underwent a transformation. He became a man again. As he dressed, his confidence returned. He generously tipped me a rupee and promised to return the following month.

I accompanied him out. At the doorway, my feet froze. Bottle in hand, a drunk Bhajan Lal was entertaining Sakhu Bai with his antics. Madam was laughing uproariously.

4

Sakhu Bai was perched on her wooden stool outside the cage, which was on the ground floor and faced the street. Since none of the regular office traffic took this notorious road, Sakhu Bai would sometimes spread a frayed *chatai* on the pavement after sunset and sprawl out comfortably. (Whenever she spread her well-worn mat, an acquaintance would invariably drop by for a chat; or perhaps whenever she got news that a guest was coming, she would spread her chatai and sit with her copper paan box next to her.)

I walked up to the door and froze in shock.

'Your next client is here,' Sakhu Bai announced from her wooden stool, gesturing to Bhajan Lal.

'Maybe. Maybe not,' I said coolly.

'He is refusing to go with any other girl except you.'

'That's his problem.'

She glanced at Bhajan Lal and then turned back to me. 'He is Babu Rao's man!' Babu Rao was perhaps some local gangster, I guessed. 'You will have to take him.'

I refused flatly.

It was two in the morning. I informed her that I had just seen my tenth and last client to the door.

'What kind of client was that!' Sakhu Bai rose from her stool. 'Was that limp-*lund chakka* even a man?'

I realized Madam had been eavesdropping; she knew what had transpired between Sadoba and me.

'Man or not, he was my tenth client. I won't take an eleventh man whether he works for a Dada or a Lala.'

As I turned to go back in, Sakhu Bai swooped on me like a hawk and grabbed my hair. I was stunned. I had not expected the old reptile to be so agile.

'*Saali, kutti*!' Bhajan Lal roared. 'This two-rupee whore behaves like gori *chamdi* from Peddar Road. Thrash her!'

Sakhu Bai began slapping me fiercely. Her grip on my hair was so strong that I felt she would tear my scalp off. I shrieked in pain. Nirmala and the twins rushed out and, after a combined struggle, they succeeded in separating me from Sakhu Bai's furious grip.

My face had turned blood red, but I didn't want to say anything to Sakhu Bai. And then Bhajan Lal began sniggering, throwing me into a mad rage.

'Fuck you! *Madarchod*, bastard!' I screamed in impotent fury. In response, he spat on my face and threatened to come back the following evening, as my first client!

But before evening came, the morning crept in, flooding me with good tidings and making me forget all my sorrows. A few days earlier, I had sent Aai a postcard. I finally got a reply.

She was alive!

I was relieved and thanked Yellamma silently.

At 10 a.m., I left the cage and trundled down the road to the Marwari's shop. Every morning, I would take part of my nightly income and deposit it at the shop. I kept a record of my savings in a pocketbook. Today, I added five rupees more to my savings and opened my little book on his desk for him to sign. Then he opened his big *pothi* of an accounts' book and informed me that I had saved Rs 110 so far. I tallied this figure with my little pocketbook. As he closed the pothi, he asked, 'So would you like to buy gold bangles or shall I show you new saris?'

I was interested neither in jewellery nor in clothes. I had all the clothes I needed and some costume jewellery for daily use. I gave him our address in the village and asked him to immediately dispatch a money order of Rs 101 to Aai.

I returned from the Marwari's shop to find Sakhu Bai sitting on the chatai, as if waiting for me.

'Come, beti. Sit with me.'

Ignoring her, I went inside. I pulled out the tin trunk from under the bed and tucked my little pocketbook between my clothes. Then I pulled out a clean sari.

My impudence must have annoyed her, but her face did not betray any emotions. It seemed like she was taking special care not to hurt my feelings. She came in and stood behind me. 'Kumud, you are a strange one! Other girls on this street go out of their way to lay as many men as they can. And here you are, refusing influential customers . . .'

I remained silent, arranging the pleats of my sari. She continued, 'Every day, three to four clients who come for you leave disappointed. On holidays, there are more than five.

Give the matter some thought. If other girls seduce them, who stands to lose?'

Hooking the last button of my blouse, I snapped, 'I don't care.'

'But why?'

'My choice.'

'Then why did you choose this profession?'

'Because this is the only profession that suits me.'

She looked at me with motherly concern. She genuinely seemed unable to comprehend me. I sat on the edge of the bed, facing her. The words just poured out of my mouth. 'I want to continue in this business. Not for years, but for decades. Like other girls, I too have the vigour to take on twenty-five men every night. But I know the fate that awaits me then. I saw my childhood friend Champa turn into a hag in the prime of her youth. Is that what you want for me?'

Sakhu Bai gawked at my face. My question hung unanswered. Perhaps no one else had explored this strategy of extending their career as a sex worker.

I ordered lunch from a restaurant nearby. Normally, I would accompany my cage sisters out to eat, but I was feeling lazy today. The delivery boy, Sattar, came in whistling with a tray that held two chapattis, dal tadka, rice and aloo-matar, and placed it on the bed before me. There was no other place to put it besides the two beds.

'What's the news, Sattar?'

Over the months, the lanky fifteen-year-old had become a friend. Our association was pure. He liked my frankness and I was drawn to his boyish innocence. Every day, he made several trips to the cages to deliver tea. Each time, he would chat with me for a few minutes before leaving with the empty cups.

Sattar pulled out a beedi stashed behind his ear, lit it and placed it between his lips. Then, taking a long drag, he started, 'Oh man! Last night, there was a massive free-for-all—'

'Where? Who?' I was hooked. He had a style of presenting neighbourhood news in a way that grabbed his listeners' attention.

'Rehmat Khan Lala's son, Dawood, and that Jat fought like demons.'

Rehmat Khan Lala was the undisputed don of Kamathipura. His word was law in its fourteen lanes. Such was the awe he inspired that even dons in other parts of the city—Laal Baag, Parel, Mahim, Bhendi Bazaar—saluted him when he passed by. Only one local gangster, a tough young fighter called Babu Rao, was beginning to challenge his supremacy.

'Jat . . . who?'

'That *dalla* who brought you here in a truck . . .'

'Bhajan Lal!'

I remembered an intoxicated Bhajan Lal's threat from last night, that he would return the next day.

'What happened then?' I asked breathlessly.

Sattar took a long drag before continuing. 'That baboon, after two pegs, began thinking he was the King Kong of Kamathipura. He picked up two boys from our restaurant and threw them as if they were dead rats. They are still recovering in J.J. Hospital. He even smashed a glass partition inside our restaurant.'

'For what? Why did he do all that?'

'He came after closing hours and ordered chicken tandoori. Of course, the boys refused him entry.'

'How did Dawood Khan enter the picture?'

Sattar lit his beedi again and continued, 'Our restaurant is owned by Rehmat Khan Lala. When the Jat started brawling with our boys, Rehmat Khan Lala's car happened to pass by. Dawood, his son, who was driving, stopped the car. As he came out, the enraged Jat, like a pagal *saand*, rushed to attack him. In a flash, Dawood pulled out his Rampuri and gave him full *kharcha-paani* . . . seven times . . . in the stomach . . . *khachak*!'

My jaws, which had been chewing on the food, were still. My eyes were as wide as saucers.

'Is he dead?'

'If he isn't, he will die soon in the hospital.'

I washed my hands in the thali. The girls, too, returned from the restaurant and shared the same news, which was spreading faster than venereal disease in Kamathipura. We talked about Bhajan Lal for a long time. I was now curious about his fate. Till sundown, no news of his death had reached us.

Before beginning work for the night, I decided to go across the road to buy paan. The shop was just around the corner, near Alfred Talkies. Nirmala accompanied me. I took a good, long look at myself in the mirror of the paan-beedi shop and was pleasantly surprised. My body had filled out nicely, but I was not plump. My complexion was not peaches and cream, but I was not unbecomingly dark either. I didn't look as celestial as an actress, but I could easily pass off for a small-time fashion model.

When we returned, chewing on the paan, Sakhu Bai declared there was a booking. This meant that one of us would be sent to the customer's place.

'Who is it?' Nirmala asked.

'Narhari . . . from Banaras.'

'Send Kumud Akka,' the twins spoke in unison.

'Why me?' I shot back.

'Because we have already been to him once,' one of them said.

'That's no reason for me to go.'

Before they could reply, Sakhu Bai stepped into the conversation. 'Kumud, there is no reason for you to refuse either. Outside jobs pay double. If you're lucky, you may get gifts and gold also.'

I began wondering why, despite all these temptations, the twins were not excited about the opportunity. There was definitely more to this then they were letting on. I refused bluntly. Madam was on the verge of losing her temper. 'Kumud!' she scolded, invoking her full authority. 'You can't have your way every time. You have to go. That is an order.'

'I won't go,' I said with rebellion in my voice.

Before things got worse, Nirmala appealed. 'Madam, no need to force her. I will go instead.'

Sakhu Bai glared at Nirmala, silencing her. I looked at Nirmala who averted her gaze and stared at the ground helplessly. I knew I had to go. There was no option. And besides an unfounded suspicion, I did not have any convincing reason to further refuse Sakhu Bai.

I took the address from her and stepped out. It was a hotel on Grant Road, not very far from Kamathipura. I decided to walk. On the way, I stopped at my regular paan-beedi shop.

As I was paying, I spotted one of the twins in the mirror. Like a spy, she was following at a safe distance. Maybe Sakhu Bai suspected that I would fly away from her stinking cage and return to my village.

I could not help but laugh to myself. Nobody had compelled me to hoist up my *lehenga* and spread my legs. Mine was not a sob story of exploitation. No anxious mother in my home town was scouring the streets to find out where her little darling had disappeared. I had willingly chosen to put my body on sale. To think that I would try to run away was absurd.

I stuffed a paan in my mouth and started walking briskly again, past an old chai-wallah who was brewing tea in a kettle with bruises on it. On equally ancient wooden benches next to him, his customers sat, smoking and chatting loudly. This chai stall was where Sattar had begun working as a delivery boy almost immediately after coming to Bombay, earning Rs 100 a month, with free boarding and lodging thrown in.

A few minutes later, I crossed the railway bridge. Soon, I was in the lobby of Hotel Neelam. I rechecked the address to ascertain the room number and went up the stairs to the room—unlucky thirteen—on the first floor.

Hotel Neelam was one of those seedy joints normally found in disreputable localities—where one didn't need ID cards or paperwork, only ready cash paid up front. The rooms were charged on an hourly basis, since few men lasted longer than that in bed.

I looked for a doorbell. Unable to find any, I knocked on the wooden door and waited. A strange odour of damp carpets and sour liquor filled the claustrophobic corridor. The hotel looked almost as decrepit as our brothel.

The door opened. A rugged man of six feet stood before me. He wore a dhoti-kurta.

'Narhari . . .?'

He nodded and stepped aside to let me into the room. I went in and sat on a chair. In front of me, on the centre table, was an open bottle of cheap liquor and glasses. The bottle was half-empty. I guessed that he had downed at least half a dozen pegs before my arrival, yet he appeared quite sober.

He shut the door, walked up to me and sat down on a chair facing me. Then he poured some liquor into an empty glass, added water and two ice cubes, and offered me the drink.

'I don't drink.' I smiled politely.

He gaped at me as if he could not understand what I had said.

'Not even a little . . .?'

I refused firmly. He put the glass back on the table and asked, 'Shall I order a cola?'

'I have paan in my mouth.'

'At least have something. I don't like drinking alone with you staring at me like an owl.'

I poured some soda into a clean glass. While I sipped on my drink, he took large swigs of the country liquor. The stench of the desi hooch was so thick that it overcame the odour of the damp carpets.

Soon, it was past midnight. He had finished the remaining half of the bottle. He rolled the empty bottle on the floor to crush a baby cockroach. Drunk by now, his inner self surfaced slowly. He spoke about everything under the sun—but the underlying point of every conversation was that all men were evil.

Finally, he uttered some gibberish about his wife who refused him sex, wiped his lips with the back of his broad hand, got up from his chair and, without warning, lifted me right off my seat. I was unnerved. He was drunk, and I do not trust men when they are drunk!

Taking two steps forward, he threw me on the bed like a sack of grain. Now I was incensed. With great effort, I suppressed the desire to slap him hard. He had paid for a pleasant evening after all.

Lying on the bed, I focused on undressing. But before I could free myself of my sari, he had taken off all his clothes and was stark naked, ready to go. He pulled my sari off, made a ball out of it and threw it into a corner. Just as brutishly, he tore off my blouse and petticoat.

Such uncouth behaviour was difficult to handle. I had never come across such a freak before. Yes, a few clients went crazy, but only after mounting me—then they would hammer me till my bones ached. But here, this gorilla had gone berserk even before doing anything. God knows how I would survive the night with this beast!

My fears came true. Half an hour later, I ran out of Hotel Neelam, my head spinning, my face ablaze with anger. My eyes felt like burning coals. From top to bottom, I was shivering with rage.

Taking long, furious strides, I reached Kamathipura. I stepped into my cage and grabbed Sakhu Bai by the neck.

She was tougher than I thought. Extricating herself, she gave me a stinging slap on the cheek and boxed me so hard on the nose that it sent me reeling. The pain was excruciating. Howling like a baby, I collapsed on the bed. I buried my face in a pillow and sobbed.

'Kumud?' Nirmala's caring voice echoed in my ears. She was in the next bed with a client. The curtains of her bed were drawn. I could not see her face but could hear her clearly.

'What did you expect?' I yelled. 'He did to me what he did to all of you!' Standing at the entrance of the cage, holding the bars, the twins giggled. Nirmala parted the curtains enough to peek through. 'Did he hurt you?'

'No. He was making bizarre demands . . . When I said no, he tried to burn my thighs with a cigarette!'

'And then?'

'I fought back!' The scene was still fresh in my mind. 'I smashed an empty liquor bottle on his head and ran as fast as I could.'

Tears welled up in my eyes. But before I broke down again, I soundly abused Sakhu Bai. 'Nirmala,' I said loudly, as if addressing only her, 'this greedy old cunt of a madam would cut us girls up and feed us to the vultures for ten rupees. She knew what a monster Narhari is, still she—'

That was all I could say before I choked. Sakhu Bai was as thick-skinned as a rhino. Neither my words, nor my tears, had any effect on her. Sitting calmly on her wooden stool, she chewed on paan like a bored old cow.

A week passed. It was as if all the life had been seeped out from my body. Again and again, I felt like running away from there, but where would I go? I consoled myself that every profession had occupational hazards. A businessman doesn't pull down the shutters at the first sign of trouble. No! A tycoon is someone who finds ways around challenges and continues to expand his empire.

I did not want to quit my profession. While that was clear to me, it was equally clear that this cage was not the right place for me any more. For the first time, it dawned on me that I was not born for the cages. I was meant for bigger things. The next step of my ladder was a numbered bungalow. How enticing those red numbers looked hanging outside the bungalows like lanterns!

Whenever I would cross Shuklaji Street at night, I would stare longingly at the bungalows with their lit signs. The windows mostly remained shut. When they were open, they were covered with curtains that had beautiful prints. It was not possible for a random passer-by to peep into the mysteries of this magical secret world, not unless one walked up the stairs with an appointment.

Some of these one-storeyed houses were also air-conditioned. If I found a place in one of these, my rate would shoot up from Rs 10 to almost Rs 50. Even the clients visiting these posh places would be considerably more refined than the working-class animals I was forced to service. I could only imagine how glamorous the girls who worked there must be. My thoughts crystallized, my target became as clear as daylight.

As I sat there thinking, Sattar entered with breakfast.

'What's up?' he said as he placed the tray on the bed. 'You seem depressed these days.'

For a second, I was unsettled by his uncanny observation. 'I have not been keeping well.'

'What's it?' he asked, lowering his voice. 'Gonorrhoea? Syphilis?'

I shook my head. 'I have been lucky so far.'

'What is it then?'

I looked around before confiding in him. 'Sattar, I am not interested in this place any more.'

'Want to go back home? To your village?'

'No. I want to move to a better place.'

'Will the old hag allow?'

'Why won't she?'

'Because she paid quite a solid price . . . full Rs 300 to buy you.'

That was a rude shock. So far, I had been under the impression that Champa had introduced me to Madam out of the pure goodness of her heart, to help me fulfil my dream. I had thought that the madam had generously given me a place in her cage after seeing my filled-out body.

'Whom did Sakhu Bai pay?' I asked Sattar cautiously.

'You had come with some girl?'

'Champa.'

'She pocketed the money and left Bombay.'

Sattar gazed at the changing expressions flitting across my face and added, 'If you are determined to leave this place, you will have to pay Rs 300 to Madam. Nobody will give you a place otherwise. That is the rule here.'

My breakfast lay untouched, the tea had gone cold. I couldn't imagine that my childhood friend, Champa, of all people, would sell me behind my back. I kept staring at Sattar blankly.

'I know how you feel,' Sattar said, trying to pull me out of my emotional shock. 'After Abba's death in the Moradabad riots, a family friend assured Ammi that he would take me to Poona to train me as a stable boy. "Someday he will become a jockey and mint money," he had said to Ammi. Instead, he sold me to a child prostitution ring. I know this pain of betrayal. But I escaped and made a life for myself in Bombay . . . One day, this will also seem like a faraway dream—a nightmare you are not even sure you dreamed.'

After Sattar left, I realized that I was not in a cage, but in a prison. I could not win my freedom unless I paid that amount. It would take me at least six months to collect Rs 300. It also meant that I would not be able to send Aai the monthly money order.

My chain of thoughts was disrupted by a stranger who had shoved his arm into my enclosure and grabbed me firmly by the wrist. Nirmala and the twins were at the municipal tap, washing their clothes. I was alone in the cage. Our madam was snoring on the adjoining bed.

When I started screaming, she woke up. 'Who's it? What happened?' she mumbled, half-asleep. Right before her eyes, a clean-shaven guy was dragging me out. She understood with a single glance at his stony face that he was a policeman in civilian clothes.

She quietly pulled the sheet over her face again and turned her back to me, as if she had not seen or heard anything. The policeman pulled me into a police van parked at the street corner. I got into the van wordlessly.

There were nine other girls inside the van. Unlike me, they did not look worried. They chatted and laughed as if this was a picnic. Some more girls were pushed inside and the doors of the police van were closed with a slam. The Black Maria sped towards the police station.

5

All of us were stuffed into a holding area at the police station. It was not cramped enough to be called a corridor, but it wasn't big enough to be called a room either. Two windows overlooked a courtyard. Inside, against the wall, was a long wooden stand in which rifles with bayonets rested in a row.

Two girls had wandered off to one of the windows, commencing a spitting match to see who could shoot paan spittle the farthest. The rest had sprawled out on the floor, chewing tobacco and gossiping loudly.

I stood alone, observing everything with bewilderment. After a few minutes, I sat down in a corner. Dark clouds of anxiety about my future began to gather. Would I be remanded to police custody? What if the magistrate decided to send me back to my village? All my grand dreams would be washed away like rainwater in a gutter.

An hour later, the door swung open and a majestic woman appeared along with a police officer. She wore a regal black sari with a golden border and held a king-sized cigarette in her long fingers. I observed her closely. Fair as an ivory statue, she radiated dignity. The room fell silent at the unspoken authority she commanded.

She then blew a lazy smoke ring as her eyes swept across the room one single time, examining the girls as casually as a customer would choose colourful birds in a pet shop. Once she was done, she closed the door gently and left with the officer.

I went up to the door to peep. The woman in the black and gold sari was seated across the tense DSP's (Deputy Superintendent of Police) desk. A rusty fan was stirring the humid air. A Hindi film song squeaked from a transistor radio somewhere. At an appropriate distance from the desk, a group of eight madams stood respectfully, a gaggle of nervous anticipation. But where was my madam?

Gradually, I got the picture. The woman in black and gold was someone influential who had been called in by the madams to bail their girls out. She was now negotiating for the girls. But what about me? The madam of my cage was not here. Maybe this was her way of exacting revenge. It would not be a surprise for me to know that she had deliberately entrapped me.

For a brief moment, I allowed myself the escape of a romantic fantasy—if only I had a lover who would come on a white horse to rescue me. A special someone in whose arms I could let go of this lonely fight. After a tiring night at work, I would welcome him inside me, to erase the pain of all the long hours spent with strangers. I snapped out of my bliss when I heard the sound of a chair being moved.

The woman had risen from her chair, and so had the DSP. I do not know what transpired between them, but he seemed almost deferential; he even offered her a polite handshake. The woman then turned to the madams who were quick to respond—they rushed into our room. Within minutes, they had swooped up their girls and left.

The woman, too, was about to leave when her eyes fell on me. Like an unclaimed body in a morgue, I too was alone within the four walls. Curious, she walked up to me slowly and peered at my face for some time, the cigarette in her fingers now a glowing stub.

'Has no one come for you?'

I shook my head.

'Where are you from?'

'Third cage on the second lane.'

'That pit-faced Sakhu Bai?'

She dropped the cigarette butt on the floor and crushed it under her heel. She appeared to be lost in thought as her eyes rested on me. I stood still with downcast eyes. At last, she came to some conclusion in her head and signalled me to follow her.

I was baffled but happy. I felt like a death-row prisoner who had been granted pardon on the eve of his hanging. Every cell in my body was thrumming with anticipation.

Outside the police station, a stately Ambassador car was waiting for us. The woman in black sat behind the wheel. I was still standing outside. She signalled me to join her. Timidly, I sat next to her. She started the engine and headed for Kamathipura.

'What's your name?'

I told her.

I wanted to know her name too but could not summon enough courage to ask. I had no clue who she was or where she was taking me. But it was enough for me to know that she wished me well and was taking me to a better life than Sakhu Bai's depressing cage.

Turning into Shuklaji Street, she asked again, 'Shall I drop you at your cage?'

I was taken aback. I did not know where I wanted to go, but returning to Sakhu Bai's cages simply didn't make sense. So I kept silent.

'You don't want to go back?'

'No.'

'Will you come to my place?'

I looked at her.

Her eyes were focused on the road ahead. The car moved slowly, negotiating both pedestrians and traffic.

I mustered up the courage to ask her a question. 'What do I have to do at your place?'

She laughed and replied. 'The same thing you did back at the old cage.'

'I don't know your name.'

She smiled warmly as she revealed it. 'Gangu Bai.'

So that's who the lady in black was—the fabled Gangu Bai. Even though Rehmat Khan Lala and Babu Rao were the two mafia dons who fought fierce battles over Kamathipura, it was Gangu Bai who reigned supreme over its fourteen streets. If they met Gangu Bai anywhere, they would bow before her. Every new police officer posted to this jurisdiction would first visit her to pay his respects. And if she ever visited the police station, senior officers would rise from their seats as if the home secretary had arrived.

Gangu Bai's establishment was in the seventh lane of Kamathipura. It could not be called a cage because it did not have a smutty ambience. There were no doors with iron bars at the entrance. It was not cramped, and unlike cages, it was not grimy. Though it was not a numbered, air-conditioned bungalow, the place was clean and hygienic with freshly painted walls. There were long benches and glossy black wooden chairs, the kind one found in decent Irani restaurants.

Gangu Bai's brothel was basically a giant warehouse packed with over a hundred and fifty girls. The establishment had two storeys. The ground floor was a large hall, while the upper floor had private rooms. These included Gangu Bai's quarters—a self-contained apartment with two rooms and a kitchen. The drawing room had a balcony that faced the road while the bedroom had an attached bathroom and toilet. She lived there alone.

Upon arriving, I was neither elated nor heartbroken. To be honest, I was a little disappointed. This flesh factory was nowhere near my aspiration of a numbered villa. On the contrary, the minute I stepped into that wholesale godown, I felt like I had lost my identity. Now I was one amongst a hundred and fifty girls. One more cow in the cowshed. However, all said and done, this place did bring some positive changes in my life.

For one, I did not have to worry about food. Whether or not the girls had clients, they were assured of two square meals and breakfast every morning, thanks to our Rajasthani cook. (Of course, his wages came out of our earnings.) Our daily income went directly to Gangu Bai, out of which she would first cut her 40 per cent commission. Only at the end of the month would we receive the remaining sixty.

I also have to admit that it was well-organized. The place had a manager, a woman called Devi, who maintained the girls' accounts. Every girl's name was registered in it. That day, one more account was opened. Mine.

In fact, the whole operation ran so smoothly and mechanically that I found myself getting bored. Days passed as slowly as a crab crawls. *I am not made for such a dreary life*—this thought began pricking me. But I was helpless. My eyes were still set on the numbered bungalows and there seemed to be no other path in sight. I had to escape this cattle shed. But first, it was essential to secure a place in a bungalow.

One evening, I was waiting for clients in this new environment. The night progressed, and with it the number of clients swelled too. The hall was packed with dhotis, trousers, pyjamas and lungis. The men would look around, pick a girl and head for one of the cubicles. Sometimes, when there were no cubicles available, the men waited for their turn, sitting on chairs with their girls on their laps—their fingers playing around with the girls' blouses. So far, not a single client had approached me. I, too, had become apathetic because I no longer had to worry about survival. There was always enough to eat and drink, and that was making me lethargic.

Midnight passed, and I was still unchosen. Just then, I spotted Sattar strutting in, all dressed up in his Eid best. My face lit up. I greeted him with a broad grin.

'Wah, Sattar!' I said, making him sit beside me. I teased him. 'No sign of a moustache on your face yet, but here you are—!'

He blushed amiably. Sattar had just entered his sixteenth year. That day, he wore a chequered, chocolate-coloured lungi below a cotton vest. He also wore a leather belt around his waist with a money pouch; I don't think he had started wearing underwear yet.

'How is Sakhu Bai?' I inquired.

'Fine . . .' he said, rolling his eyes.

Since the night I had entered the seventh lane, I had not stepped out. Truth be told, I did not feel like going out. Otherwise, my old cage was a ten-minute walk away; I could have dropped in to meet my old friend, Nirmala.

'And what else is happening?'

'Bhajan Lal is on life support.'

'He isn't dead yet?'

'If he dies, Babu Rao won't rest till he settles the score with Lala.'

'Why? What do you mean?'

'Bhajan Lal works for Babu Rao. And Dawood, who gutted his stomach like a pomfret, is Lala's son. Anyway, a war between the two gangs has been on the boil for a while now. We are gearing for a full-scale assault with choppers on our restaurant in the next few days.' He then remembered something and reached for the pouch on his belt, fishing out a soiled envelope.

'What's this?'

'This letter was delivered for you at Sakhu Bai's address.'

A glance at the envelope was enough to set my heart aflutter—the letter was from Tulu, from Aai. Hurriedly, I tore it open and read the letter in a single breath. Its contents made me feel overjoyed: Aai wanted to visit Bombay. She wrote that she had been receiving all my money orders regularly. Apart from this, she had written to say that her body was not resilient like before, that the drought had ended but its toll on her health had persisted.

Aai's letter created a new predicament, albeit a sweet one. If Aai came to Bombay, I would have to arrange for her stay, ideally where I was or someplace close by because her health was not robust. For that, I would have to seek Gangu Bai's permission. What if she refused?

That night, Sattar proved to be a good luck charm. After he left, I attracted seven clients one after the other and tried my best to give them the taste of paradise they deserved and had paid for.

My simple rule was to be grateful to the man who chose me, who spent his hard-earned money on me—to ensure that he got what he paid for, and a little more. If he asked for a cigarette, I would give him a cigarette and a lighter. Total submission to his gratification was my secret. Prostitutes in Kamathipura, however, were mostly cheats, frauds and swindlers. Their rule was to give the man as little as possible. Some blatantly picked their clients' pockets during sex. Others deliberately made first-timers ejaculate within seconds and picked their pockets more discreetly.

It was midnight, the perfect time to meet Gangu Bai. She slept most of the day and her mornings would dawn only at noon. She would have a leisurely breakfast in bed, listening to the radio and reading the newspapers. After an hour in the bath, she would put on a dazzling new sari. Only then would she greet the world. After all, she wasn't called the queen of Kamathipura for nothing!

I climbed the stairs to the first floor, imagining Gangu Bai to be sitting all alone or chatting with someone. My guess was completely wrong.

Her door was ajar. Peeping into her drawing room, I discovered a smoky gambling den in operation. Clouds of cigarette smoke and echoes of drunk laughter wafted outside from those sitting at a round table scattered with plastic counters, playing cards and pegs of liquor. Gangu Bai, surrounded by five men, was the only woman in the group.

I was uncertain whether to knock or not. Three of the men had their backs to the door, so I could not see their faces. The other two were across the round table, facing me, along with Gangu Bai who looked imperious in a royal blue sari.

The man sitting next to her caught my attention. There was something peculiar about his face. He sported a rugged moustache, like an old-time Indian wrestler, and had a prominent birthmark on his right cheek. His jaw was as square as a granite block. He had a crew cut and wore a white safari suit. His arms were muscled and his chest was so broad that the top of the suit was plastered to his body like second skin.

Gangu Bai tossed an unwanted card on the table and then looked at him meaningfully. 'Rao, pick it up, it's your lucky day.'

Was this Rehmat Khan Lala's sworn rival Babu Rao?

'My queen,' he smirked, casting a cursory glance at Gangu Bai before picking up another card from the deck.

'The day you pass the right card to me, I will announce from the rooftops that the old don is dead and Rao is the godfather of Kamathipura.'

My guess was correct. This tough guy was indeed the same Babu Rao—Lala's enemy No. 1 and the owner of nine opium dens in Kamathipura. Sattar had told me that he also made a sizeable commission on smuggled goods coming in from Dubai.

The card Babu Rao had picked up from the deck proved to be useless. He threw it back on the table. Standing behind the half-closed door, I wondered if I should come another time to seek an audience with Gangu Bai . . .

Her eyes fell on me. I felt like a petty thief caught red-handed, and a chill ran down my spine. I was seized by a sudden desire to run away, to lose myself in the crowd downstairs, but my leaden feet would not cooperate.

'Who's it?' Gangu Bai called out from her chair.

'Me . . . It's me, Kumud,' I answered as I opened the door and stepped in.

'Where's Devi?'

'I will fetch her right away.'

'Tell her I am still waiting for the two bottles of soda and a plate of wafers.'

I left the room at once.

I went around and looked into a few rooms to find Devi. Finally, I found her in the kitchen. When she saw me, she said, 'Take these soda bottles and potato chips to Maa's room. I will get these prawns as soon as they are fried.'

Devi was not the only one who called Gangu Bai 'Maa'. All the girls in Kamathipura addressed her as their mother.

This time, I walked into Gangu Bai's room without hesitation. They had packed up the card game. Another round of drinks was about to commence. I quietly placed the soda bottles and wafers on the side table beside Gangu Bai's armchair. There were two bottles of whisky in the room; one was almost half-empty. Gangu Bai picked up that bottle and poured some whisky into each glass.

'Kumud,' she said without looking at me, as she opened the soda bottle. 'Are you happy here?'

'Yes.'

'No problems?'

Eyes lowered, I shook my head.

After she had finished pouring soda into everyone's glass, she looked up. 'You wanted to say something?'

'Yes . . .' This was the perfect time. I gathered all my courage and managed to blurt out, 'I received a letter from home, from Aai . . . my mother . . . wants to come to Bombay for a visit . . . a short visit.'

'When is she expected?'

'Next week.'

'No problem,' she said affectionately, taking a sip from her glass. 'Just inform Devi. She will make all the necessary arrangements. Anything else?'

I was beside myself with joy. No wonder all the girls in these disreputable lanes looked up to her and called her their mother—she was truly maternal in the way she treated us. Every Diwali, she would gift all her girls a brand new sari. If any girl under her roof fell sick or contracted an STD, she would bear the entire responsibility, including paying the bills for her treatment. When a prostitute became too old to entertain, she was retired with a respectable pension. Prematurely burned-out or frustrated girls who wanted to go back home were provided with railway tickets and a food packet for the journey. If people called her the queen of Kamathipura, they were not wrong. She deserved it. Perhaps even the Queen of England did not take care of her subjects the way she did.

As the days passed, Gangu Bai's brothel began to grow on me. I found my own customers too—a loyal clientele of around twenty-five men. Three of them came practically every night. The rest visited me once a fortnight or so.

Moreover, some of my old clients from Sakhu Bai's cage learnt of my new address and began to drop in too. But I held firm to my principle of not accepting more than ten clients a night. Little did I know that in Kamathipura, principles among whores were as dangerous as honesty among the cops. And my principles would put me in direct conflict with none other than Babu Rao.

6

The evening that Aai arrived from Satara was the same night that Bhajan Lal met his twisted Maker. For two days, he had been in critical condition, on a ventilator, at J.J. Hospital. At last, that night, he stopped breathing forever.

His death evoked neither sorrow nor elation in me. The first step in the ladder of my journey in Kamathipura had given way. I was now standing securely on the third step; the second step had been Sakhu Bai's cage. I had no doubt that a numbered bungalow would be my fourth. I believed in slowly but surely taking one step at a time. Unlike other girls, I did not fantasize about miraculous happy endings.

Just the exterior of Gangu Bai's brothel was enough to render Aai awestruck. She had spent her entire life in the wretched village of Tulu. She had known neither peace nor prosperity. All night she would thirst for clients, yet none would knock at her door. And the drought had only made it worse—in its final days, even her lover, Constable Naik, had deserted her.

Aai had brought a corroded tin trunk that held all her earthly belongings—her clothes, her combs, her make-up and her memories. I guided her to her room. With Gangu Bai's blessing, she had been allotted a room on the first floor—the floor which housed Gangu Bai's apartment, as well as five dorms for the girls. A daytime crèche for the fatherless children of the prostitutes was also located on this floor, besides a couple of guest rooms. Fortunately, I was allowed to stay in one of these rooms with Aai.

Aai bathed and changed into a fresh sari. It was four-thirty in the evening. There were still a couple of hours to go before the loins of men sprang to life. I organized masala chai and idli-sambar with green chutney for Aai, and sat beside her while she wolfed it down. So far, besides the formal greetings and small talk, we hadn't touched upon anything significant. I watched her while she drank the steaming hot brew from the cutting glass. There were dark circles under her eyes and her face looked washed out, like an old wall that has been beaten pale by decades of rain lashing against it. Her body was in even worse repair.

'Aai, look at your condition . . . Your body has been reduced to a sack of bones. You've shrunk to half your size!'

She set her empty glass down and offered a pale smile. 'Beti, it seems as if Goddess Yellamma has stripped me bare and taken all I had to make you blossom. When you left the village, how skinny you were! And look at you now! Seeing your bright cheeks, our apples would die of shame.' She paused here for a while and then, taking a deep breath, continued, 'For a few days, let these failing eyes be filled with the sight of you and fresh blood will begin coursing in my sagging body too.'

'And,' I inquired with a smile, 'after that?'

'You want to keep me here?'

'What's in the village to go back for?'

She pushed away the empty plate and glass, dabbing her lips with the loose end of her sari.

'I forgot to mention. Constable Naik's wife and three sons perished in the drought, but his daughter survived. I have taken her in.'

'Kumkum?' I distinctly remembered the large-eyed girl with wild, brown hair.

'She is around twelve-thirteen and will begin earning in a few years. Rest assured, I will be able to spend my last days in peace.'

'Will she agree to enter our trade?'

'Why won't she?'

'She is not from our lineage.'

'But she is a woman!' Aai shot back confidently. 'And every woman longs for more than one man. All she needs is an opportunity. Once she tastes blood, there will be no going back.'

I was flabbergasted by Aai's observation.

Soon, pale bulbs casting feeble yellow light came to life, one after another. It was time for business at the brothel. I asked Aai to rest while I dressed for the night. That night was special for me because Aai was there. I wore my favourite baby pink sari with delicate silver zari work and applied sandalwood oil as I parted my thick hair. Unlike the other girls, I never needed too much make-up. My skin naturally glowed like honey.

I fixed a fresh jasmine gajra into my braid and stepped out of the room. I walked past Gangu Bai's rooms and had just put my hand on the banister to take the stairs when I saw Babu Rao climbing up. His skin was swarthy and his face looked darker in his starched white safari suit.

I took a step back to the first-floor landing and flattened myself against the wall to make way for him. He clomped up all the way, but instead of turning towards Gangu Bai's quarters he stopped near me. We were now face to face. I could see the birthmark under his right eye. He began examining me in a way that made me uncomfortable. His gaze, which had reached my feet, now slithered upward. Pausing for an extra few seconds around my breasts, he licked the corner of his mouth and looked into my eyes.

'Your name is Kumud?'

I nodded.

'Don't go to bed after the tenth client,' he declared before leaving. 'Tonight, I will be your eleventh.'

Without waiting for me to respond, he walked off to Gangu Bai's quarters. I gaped blankly behind him. Someone was challenging the principles I lived by, just to provoke me, to remind me that who I was had not changed.

My rates had improved since I had settled in Gangu Bai's warehouse. I used to charge two rupees a shot when I sold my body on the pavement. It was hiked to seven rupees when I entered pockmarked Sakhu Bai's cage. With Gangu Bai, my rate had jumped. The higher rates had nothing to do with me; I was the same Kumud who used to operate from the dark alleys a year before—this was the fixed rate for all of Gangu Bai's girls. I was worth Rs 22 now.

Babu Rao, on the other hand, was filthy rich. Moreover, his name struck terror in every corner of Kamathipura.

Not giving in to his wish—or rather, his command—meant not just questioning his authority but directly challenging it.

As I descended the stairs, I considered whether or not I should stick to my principles or surrender to a sadistic whim. As these words hammered around in my mind, a thought struck me—*how did he know so much about me? How did he know that amongst the thousands of girls in Kamathipura, a girl named Kumud refused the eleventh customer, no matter what? Bhajan Lal? Sakhu Bai? Gangu Bai? Or someone else?*

I had no answer. But I resolved to defy Babu Rao's cruel dare with all my might. I would do everything in my power to stick to what I believed in. All her life, Aai had held her chin up to every injustice thrown her way. I would not run away either.

When I entered the hall that night, it was swarming. I figured that it was the first of the month, payday for salaried employees. The first week of every month was peak season in Kamathipura—even the ugliest girl found customers during those days. And every girl tried to rake in as much cash as possible by lifting her skirt for as many men as she could.

Some girls showed zero restraint. Hard cash was all that mattered. If that meant being battered by a battalion in a single night, they would say yes without a second thought. On peak nights, some girls would even place bets—the one who bedded the maximum men by the end of the night would be declared the winner! Once, a girl from our warehouse, Juhi, took on sixty men in a single night and set the record for Kamathipura. Like a machine, she was at it from six in the evening till four in the morning, spreading her legs for half a dozen men every hour.

That night was a double bonanza—it was the first of May, and a bank holiday as well. Pockets were burning with fresh currency notes, itching to be spent. Our warehouse had a hundred and fifty girls and more than two hundred ravenous men had stormed in. The crowd was thickening with every passing minute. The queues that formed outside the cubicles were as long as those outside the single block of toilets at Churchgate railway station during rush hour. Just like a man rushed out of a public urinal after pissing, men were being tossed out one after another by the girls.

A few girls were strutting around hopefully in the middle of the warehouse. Some men sat on benches arranged along the walls, their chosen girl on their lap—like classical musicians doing *riyaaz*—before they found an empty cabin. All the plywood cabins were occupied with frenetic, fleshy action. Ten to fifteen minutes was all a client was allowed during peak hours. If the door failed to open after time was up, Devi would rattle it so violently that the client would jump out of bed in alarm!

Before I could find a spot in the bustling crowd, a youth with a shy smile approached me hesitantly. I could not place him, though he did look familiar. He was not one of my regulars, but he wasn't a stranger either. Why did my heart gladden upon seeing him? And then the next moment his name formed on my lips.

'Sadoba!'

Yes, it was Sadoba, not yet twenty years old. He sported a jaunty yellow shirt and dark brown trousers. The black shoes on his feet had the shine of freshly polished leather. I remembered him clearly now—the affable kid with neatly parted hair who had visited me at Sakhu Bai's cages. Despite my best efforts, he had failed to score and had left with his confidence shaken.

I welcomed him with a smile and looked around for a place to sit. Not a single chair was available. The doors of all the cabins were shut too. I led him to a bench, the entire length of which was occupied by a girl and her amorous client, and got the intertwined twosome to make room for us.

Sadoba sat down edgily. Unlike other men, he lacked the courage to grab me and pull me on to his lap. I had to do it myself. I sat on his thighs and threw my arms around his neck. I could tell from the broad smile that spread across his face that he appreciated it.

I had to start the conversation. 'Tell me, Sadoba, where have you been gallivanting all this while?'

'Um . . . My college exams got over last week,' he said, sliding his hand around my waist tentatively.

'Is that true?'

He nodded.

'Or were you busy seeing other girls behind my back?'

'No-o-o.'

I pouted as if I was not convinced. Then I dramatically took his left hand and placed it on my breast, saying, 'You know my heart will stop beating if you lie, don't you?'

He was obviously electrified by this move.

With every passing minute, I could sense seeds of confidence germinating within him. His hand, which had been lying limp on my breasts, now moved along slyly to find a way into my blouse and touch my nipples. 'Are you in a hurry, *jaanu?*' I chided him tenderly, making him self-conscious.

The moment a cabin door opened, I took his wrist and walked into it swiftly. This, too, was unusual. Normally, excited clients would drag the girls behind them. Sometimes, if the client was a regular, both would enter the cabin together, hand in hand. But a customer being dragged in by a girl was certainly rare.

I closed the door behind us.

Our plywood cabins were so tiny that you could touch both walls if you stretched out your hands. In the name of furniture, it had just a bed. A table fan stood on a stool in one corner. Near the fan was a small washing area with an outlet for dirty water—a *mori*. On the wall to the right of the mori was a round mirror, cracked in two places. Apart from that, if there was anything worth mentioning, it was a cheap photo frame of the Father of the nation, Mahatma Gandhi, grinning approvingly.

Sadoba sat nervously on the bed, his feet dangling. Given the crowd outside, I had limited time on my hands. In those few minutes, I had to warm him up and ensure that he derived his money's worth of pleasure. I sincerely did not want him to leave with his desire unquenched, like the previous time.

Sitting face to face, I lifted my blouse and my breasts sprang out. He gaped at them like a kid in a Diwali toy sale. His right hand gingerly slid upward from my waist and started touching a nipple, as if for the first time. I gathered my arms around him and guided his face to my breasts. His mouth was hungry on my firm nipples, and he began sucking like a baby. I could feel the warmth of his nervous breath on my skin. I began to synchronize my breathing with his ragged breaths, an old tantric trick Aai had taught me, to increase sexual pleasure. My lips explored his cheeks and neck. I held his earlobe between my teeth and bit gently. The pain aroused him further. I could feel his manhood beginning to assert itself. He was all set.

Gently, I disengaged myself from him. I swiftly undid the buttons of his trousers and began pulling his trousers down. His flagpole leapt out joyfully, the flag flying high and proud. Now he did not have the patience to even get out of his pants. His manhood ablaze, all of a sudden, he pinned me to the bed. I quickly pulled up my petticoat and lowered my panties for him. He crouched between my thighs, knees digging into the bed. I placed my hands on his buttocks to guide him to the right place. First-timers tended to wander around as if they were playing drunken darts. He stiffened his back, ready to push his manhood inside. I closed my eyes and braced for the thick heat of his erection. But . . . nothing happened. Instead, I heard a bewildered animal wail. I opened my eyes in alarm. His back was arched in spasms as he emptied himself helplessly over my thighs and navel. In his excessive excitement, the poor boy had ejaculated prematurely!

By two in the morning, I was done with all my clients. The thought of Babu Rao—and his sadistic challenge— returned to my mind. It was difficult to sneak back into the guest room without attracting his attention. I decided to ignore him in case he spotted me and march ahead to Aai.

I padded up the stairs and reached the first floor. Gangu Bai's door was closed. I could not tell if anyone was inside. There was no sound. I stopped for a moment and strained to listen. I could hear nothing. I put my ear to the door to discern any faint, fidgety scuffling within. Nothing. Perhaps

Babu Rao had forgotten. He must have more important things on his mind. I heaved a sigh of relief. As I stepped away, I spotted Devi coming out of Aai's room.

'You!' she exclaimed, glaring at me. 'You are here?'

I looked at her questioningly.

'I have been looking for you all over the place!' She threw open the doors to Gangu Bai's drawing room. I looked in. Babu Rao was sitting on a chair all alone, his elbows leaning on the round card table. The solitary bulb hanging overhead cast deep shadows around him. There was a bottle of whisky in front of him; it was nearly empty. A half-filled glass was kept beside him, but he was gazing glassy-eyed at the ruby-red drink in the bottle, for no apparent reason. When the door opened, he whipped his head around and fixed his bloodshot eyes on my face.

'What are you thinking?' Devi asked, as she shoved me into the room. 'He's been waiting for an hour!'

I silently cursed Devi as she shut the door behind me. I looked ahead. Here I was, all alone in Gangu Bai's room, face to face with a fearsome beast named Babu Rao. He drunkenly tried to stand up. His jerky movements, however, upset the chair and it tumbled down with a hollow clatter.

A shiver travelled down my shoulder blades. For a few seconds, he stood still, steadying himself. Then he lumbered across, one heavy step at a time, around the upturned chair, to me. I had gathered my wits by now and was mentally prepared to face him.

He was drunk out of his skull. The smooth birthmark on his right cheek shone in the yellow light of the bulb. His moustache made him look even more villainous. He laid his paw-like hands on my shoulders and pulled me towards him. His hands slid down to grip my waist.

I could smell his sour breath on my face when his lips moved at last. 'You don't like me?'

I was surprised. His voice was not as severe as his face.

'I don't accept more than ten customers in a night . . .'

'Not even me?'

I shook my head.

'What if I force myself on you?'

'That would be rape.'

Though he was drunk, he burst out laughing. The word 'rape' from a prostitute's mouth was hilarious for him.

'Rani was right,' he said. 'You are one stubborn bitch . . . and I don't want any rabid bitches in my territory.'

And then, suddenly, he hooked his fingers into my blouse and ripped it apart. I was stunned! He then spun me around and slammed my head on the card table. The crash was so loud that I half-expected someone to come to my rescue. But, of course, I knew no one would. From behind, he lifted my baby pink sari and tore my underwear.

What followed next can only be classified as rape. I have no other words to verbalize it. That incident remains buried in a black hole in my memory, beyond the words and grammar of ordinary life. A hole marked by a single gravestone, a single stark word on it—Rape.

Half an hour later, Babu Rao was sitting on his chair. He emptied whatever whisky was left in the bottle, drinking it neat. I stood sobbing quietly on the other side of the card table. Through glistening eyes, I looked at the crushed mogra buds from my torn gajra, now scattered all over the floor.

My back was turned towards him as I fumbled to cover my breasts with my tattered blouse. No matter how much I tried, I failed. It made me feel even more helpless. I wanted to scream, even bang my head on the wall—anything to give an outlet to my impotent fury. But I controlled myself. Doing that would mean giving him the victory he wanted—in fact, he already believed he had won.

But a wounded woman's attack can be more venomous than a snake. It was my turn now. I took a deep breath and turned my tear-stained face towards him. He was watching me with a triumphant smirk. This was the perfect time to puncture his pompous pride.

'What are you thinking?' Babu Rao murmured. For a second, I was again taken aback by the gentleness in his voice. Was he planning to rape me again? I didn't care any more.

'Rao,' I said, my tear-choked voice lethal and cutting, 'you were my tenth client tonight. If you want to be my eleventh, try again tomorrow.'

He was thunderstruck. It took the poison of my words a few seconds to enter his bloodstream and find a way to his heart. He gaped at me with desperate, betrayed eyes. Before his alcohol-fogged brain could compose a reply, I walked out of the room.

Aai was fast asleep on the bed in our room. I lay my sore body down on the stiff mattress on the floor. I curled my body under the sheet, but sleep eluded me. Somewhere in

Kamathipura, a clock struck four. My brain was rattled with humiliation.

Till that day, I had only heard stories of rape. Back in Tulu, a girl who had been sexually abused by her stepfather had lost her voice—she had become mute, as if to protest the unspeakable act. I had sympathized, but I had not experienced her agony. Today, I felt it as if it was my own. Her lips pressed against each other in furious silence were my own. My eyes brimmed with tears again.

No doubt, I had mentally prepared myself for this encounter. I had slept with nine clients instead of my usual ten. I knew Babu Rao would resort to brute force to make me give in. But I did not want to submit to his sadistic whims so easily. Who was Babu Rao! Kamathipura feared him as a goonda, a future underworld don perhaps. But for me, he was merely a man. Actually, not even that. He was a pompous worm with an overblown ego. Till the end, he had been under the delusion that he had crushed me under his boot, as he had done with so many others. But before leaving, I had hit back where it hurt the most. He would be the one writhing in pain now—like a snake cut into half.

7

It had been a week since Aai had been in Bombay, yet she had not stepped out of the brothel. She had not even expressed the desire to do so. This had its benefits though—a much-needed respite of one week, along with two square meals, had rekindled the glow on her face.

It was Sunday. I decided to take Aai sightseeing. I had woken up early as well. Usually, my eyes did not open before half-past eleven, but today it was not even ten.

I was lazing on the bed, yawning. Aai had washed her hair—it glistened as she spread a frayed chatai in a sunlit pool by the window and sat cross-legged on it. I watched as she chewed on her double-egg omelette with stiff pav and butter. Wisps of steam curled over her tea perched by the window.

After breakfast, she began fussing with her silver paan-daan to make herself the first paan of the day. Smearing the freshly washed betel leaf with white chuna and red kattha paste, she took out a tiny box from the silver box. From that, she extracted a pinch of chewing tobacco and some chopped betel nuts, and sprinkled them on the leaf. Folding the betel leaf carefully into a triangle, she put it into her mouth.

'You didn't sleep well today?' Aai asked, noticing me observe her, as she snapped the lid of the silver box shut.

'Because I have to take you sightseeing today, no? First we will visit the world-famous Chowpatty beach. The Hanging Gardens are nearby. I will take you there as well.'

'Now?' asked Aai, dubiously gesturing to the blinding summer sun outside.

I raised myself from the bed. 'Don't you know your darling daughter works the evening shift?'

'Can't my daughter take a day off for her dearest mother?' she shot back with a smile.

Aai was right. I was surprised it hadn't occurred to me before.

'Why not!' I said.

At four that evening, a horse-drawn Victoria pulled up outside the brothel. I had struck a deal with the coachman—three hours for twenty rupees.

As our Victoria crossed the seventh lane of Kamathipura and entered the second lane, I caught sight of Sattar. He was sitting on a wooden box outside a barbershop, trying to read an Urdu newspaper. I signalled the coachman to halt and called out to him.

'Are you free?' I asked, proposing three fun-filled hours. In response, he tossed the newspaper aside and jumped into the hutch of the horse carriage.

Sattar told me that he was no longer working at the restaurant owned by Rehmat Khan Lala. For seven years, he had slogged there like a slave. And he had recently got his due—with the blessings of Rehmat Khan Lala, he had been transferred to one of his liquor dens. The pay was higher and the working hours shorter. At the restaurant, he used to work like a mule from six in the morning to eleven at night. At the liquor joint, he worked for just eight hours, from seven in the evening till two at night. That seemed funny to me— the working hours of prostitutes were the same. While the rest of Bombay slept, Kamathipura's legs were wide open for business. I had not realized that our odd hours provided a boost to other businesses as well.

Aai and I had to squeeze into the broad back seat. Sattar sat facing us, silently puffing on a beedi. I noticed his face had matured. A silky wisp of a moustache had begun to make its appearance. I also noticed that—for the first time—he was stealing glances at my cleavage.

The Victoria turned left from the Grant Road traffic lights. Crossing Lamington Road, we proceeded towards Opera House. Aai was mesmerized by the metropolis. Google-eyed, she was taking in every single object— enormous glass-fronted emporiums with crystal chandeliers inside, skyscrapers with hundreds of windows, shiny motor cars with stylishly dressed women inside . . . For a middle-aged woman who had never stepped out of Tulu, these sights were captivating. But it was a glimpse of Chowpatty beach that really took her breath away.

Water! Water as far as the eye could see. Water touching the sky. Water so vast that her life and its problems felt small and insignificant. I had also been engulfed by the same sense of wonderment when I had seen the ocean for the first time. I had remembered the wide Krishna river that passed through our village. All through my childhood it had seemed so impossibly wide. Yet, compared to the majesty of the Arabian Sea, it was just a humble village stream.

The Victoria stopped on the pavement opposite Wilson College. Aai wanted to feel the sand under her feet. After strolling barefoot on the beach for a while, we found ourselves a tree under which we could stretch our legs.

There were still two hours to go before sunset. It was May and the days were long. The air was humid, but thanks to a whipping sea breeze, it didn't feel muggy. As we sat on the sand with our legs stretched, Aai opened her paan-daan for the second round of paan.

'Sattar,' I asked casually, 'what's happening to your Dawood Khan since the Bhajan Lal incident?'

Sattar, who had been lost in his own reverie, blinked and blurted, 'Oh! He's in the lockup.'

'Since when?'

'Since the day Bhajan Lal died.'

'So now? What next?'

'He should be out on bail soon.'

After I asked Sattar a few more questions, I got a broad idea of the sequence of events. The day after Dawood had stabbed Bhajan Lal, he had gone underground. The cops had not bothered to search for him because Rehmat Khan Lala had most of the top police officers on his payroll. But there were a couple of officers under Babu Rao's patronage too, and he had tipped off one such officer about Dawood's hideout. Rehmat Khan Lala had obviously suspected Babu Rao's hand but did not have enough evidence. He deployed men to gather information and soon had proof of Babu

Rao's complicity. Babu Rao had made the mistake of poking Rehmat Khan Lala's family to balance the killing of his foot soldier, Bhajan Lal. So now this was no more a routine gang skirmish: this was a call to arms.

Rehmat Khan Lala had flown into a violent Pathan rage. Eyes bloodshot, he had cursed Babu Rao and sworn revenge, but before he could let his fury loose, he checked himself. Lala wasn't the kind to act in the heat of passion. He would first uncover his opponent's weaknesses. Then he would study the battlefield before devising a strategy. Patiently, he would wait to execute a perfectly timed attack that would fall like a thunderbolt.

Over the past few days, a nagging anxiety had been churning in my stomach. There was no telling when Babu Rao would ambush me again. In fact, I had been wondering why I had not seen him since the rape, how come he had not returned to avenge the insult I had thrown at him. Sattar's words dispelled my fears. For a few more days, Babu Rao would be fully occupied. He was pulling every string he could to ensure that Dawood remained behind bars. Unless Dawood got a life sentence, Rao would not consider that he had properly avenged Bhajan Lal's murder.

For Kamathipura's ganglords, the only way to sustain their existence was revenge. Even if Babu Rao could get Dawood sentenced for a couple of years, it would enhance his stature. The pointy tips of his moustache would stand higher.

The paans were ready. Aai offered Sattar and me a paan each, and stuffed the third into her own mouth. Chewing paan, we sat on the sandy beach a while longer. I could observe contentment on Aai's face—the contentment of my progress, happiness and prosperity.

But I had not yet made it to the air-conditioned bungalows I wished for so intensely. A shimmering thought passed through my mind—if fortune favoured me and I managed to move to a numbered bungalow, my rate would jump to Rs 50. How radiant would Aai's face look then!

After resting for half an hour, we strolled on the cool sand for a few minutes before climbing into the Victoria again. Weaving around Malabar Hill, we reached the Hanging Gardens, perched upon its peak.

The hilltop offers a breathtaking panorama of the entire metropolis—the majestic chimneys of the cotton mills and Rajabai Clock Tower, the roofs of old colonial-era mansions and the soaring new towers, green mushroom-like treetops and the flat gold blankets of sand lining the aquamarine sea glinting with fishing trawlers.

Once again, Aai's eyes fell still, as if she wanted to capture the city in her eyes. I kept glancing at her face. Only her eyes felt alive. The rest of her deeply lined face was expressionless. Fiery lava had once erupted from this volcano where there was only lifeless stone now.

At 6.30 p.m., we decided to head back. I asked the coachman to take the Alankar Cinema route through Foras Road (aka Falkland Road), the main street running across Kamathipura. This street offered Aai a different and unique panorama—both sides of this broad street, as far as the eye could see, were lined with hundreds of cages bubbling with life.

After Partition, the population of India had surged overnight due to migration, leading to a sudden shortage of accommodation. This had forced many middle-class families to reluctantly move into Kamathipura. So, this locality had some antiquated chawls too in which decent working-class families lived amongst prostitutes—and some decent middle-class chawls within which prostitutes ran a thriving business.

Here, there were one-storeyed houses, two-storeyed buildings and a few structures that were three or four storeys high as well. In the houses that had two floors, the upper floor had large, grilled windows touching the floor. At these windows, fair-skinned Nepalese girls could be seen standing, coquettishly swirling their skirts. Sitting on stools at other windows were chocolate-coloured girls from the south. Touching their noses to the bottom of some window grills were Maharashtrian girls who lay on their bellies, leaning on their elbows and cupping their chins in their hands.

For Aai, it was a fairyland. She had never seen so many sex workers in one place. Each cage contained a mouth-watering candy to which customers thronged like flies. Such a large and joyous crowd—resounding with drunken laughter, clattering bangles and bicycle rings—did not even gather for the annual fair back in the village.

Taking a U-turn at Alfred Talkies, the Victoria crossed Taj Talkies and turned the corner into Shuklaji Street. The sun had set and the evening sky was streaked with brilliant strokes of freshly painted orange and purple. Sattar jumped off the moving Victoria when we passed through the second lane. It was already 6.55 p.m. and he was supposed to report for work before seven.

'Who is that boy?' Aai asked, speaking for the first time that evening. I told her about Sattar.

'He has a soft corner for you. How old is he?'

'Around sixteen.'

'Should be ripe in a year or so, isn't it?'

I did not understand her words. But after pondering over it for a few moments, I grasped what she had actually meant: I was again shaken by Aai's astute observation. She was suggesting that I was trying to transform a raw mango like Sattar—with the warmth of my affection and favours—into a ripe one. When he was ready, I would squeeze him dry. This was not unusual in Kamathipura. An older prostitute often took a younger boy under her wing and supported him emotionally and financially to extend her youthfulness.

To be honest, I had not entertained any such thoughts about Sattar till now. Perhaps I did have a small crush on him and Aai's experienced eyes had spotted it. *Was I suppressing my true feelings for him?*

Before I could give the matter any serious consideration, the Victoria stopped at the entrance of our brothel. I paid the coachman Rs 20 and got off. Next to our brothel was the clinic of a Chinese dentist, whose name was Li Min. The shutters were being pulled down for the day. The dentist's servant heaved the accumulated waste of the day out on the street. In the bloody mixture, I saw half a dozen teeth.

I was fond of experimenting with my dressing style. On some days, I wore bell-bottoms and a boisterous floral shirt, while on other days I dressed in a more sedate Punjabi salwar-kameez. On weekends, I wore a miniskirt with a tight choli top, and on festival nights a traditional sari. Today, I put on a skirt with a coffee-coloured T-shirt that had a single word printed on it in bold white letters: 'WOW!'

I took Aai's blessings and stepped out of the room. On the way to the stairs, I passed Gangu Bai's unlocked door. I was surprised to see that amongst the guests who had come to play cards was Rehmat Khan Lala.

I couldn't get a clear view of his face as the door was only open a crack, but a glance was enough to identify him. He had no moustache but sported an immaculately trimmed inch-long beard. With a navy blue suit, he wore a tie that fell gracefully down his broad chest.

As I descended the stairs, I wondered how Babu Rao and Rehmat Khan Lala would react if they accidentally came face to face with each other here. Would they growl or smile cordially?

In the gang war, Gangu Bai's warehouse was neutral territory. Enemies visited, as did friends. Police officers and gangsters both showed up, along with government officials and common citizens. Hindus, Muslims, Christians— regardless of their faith, everyone came to find salvation here.

Such was Gangu Bai's unquestionable authority that all those who entered her domain obeyed her rules. Only she knew how many battles she had fought to earn the throne of the sovereign Queen of Whores.

I knew only a little about Gangu Bai's past. She was originally from Gujarat. They say she had come to Bombay all alone and fallen in love with Usman Dada, a middling rowdy from the Ghadiyal Godi dock area. Usman was not a ganglord, he was a petty thief—his speciality was pilfering precious items from cargo ships that docked with goods from the Middle East and African countries. With his help, Gangu Bai started a small cage in Kamathipura. She did not solicit customers herself—she invested Usman's illicit earnings to buy seven girls.

Years rolled by. Usman went for a pilgrimage to Mecca and never returned; a sandstorm in the desert not only killed him, it also buried him alive. Gangu Bai was relieved. Now, she had a hundred and fifty girls in her warehouse. Like an octopus, her reach extended to every corner in the metropolis.

Beyond the police department, she wielded influence in every branch of the city's administration. When required, she could march into the secretariat as if she owned the government. Initially, I wondered why a minister would ever fall at the feet of a whore. The mystery cleared with the passage of time.

Gangu Bai controlled the votes of Kamathipura. She could single-handedly ensure the victory of any candidate, regardless of his political party. She could also single-handedly destroy the chances of candidates she did not approve of. No wonder then that occasionally Gangu Bai's den hosted present and potential political leaders. When she was urgently required to attend a meeting, even the municipal commissioner sent attendants with a car to escort her.

Swaying my hips, I reached the hall. There was still time for the crowd to gather. Amidst all the girls, only twenty-odd clients were present. Constellating in groups on benches and chairs, the girls were in high spirits, chirping like happy birds.

The cabins were unoccupied. Men who came in early were in no hurry to get into the cubicles. Generally, clients who came at this time preferred to sit the girls on their laps and extend foreplay for as long as they could. I could see a few such couples languorously exploring each other's curves and crevices.

I was just scanning the area for a place to sit when a skinny tapori, out of nowhere, appeared before me. The next moment, he had slipped his hand around my waist and was leading me to a chair, humming a song. I was prepared for a few minutes of fondling, but I was mistaken. He passed the chairs and pulled me directly into a cabin. I did not mind. In fact, I preferred such 'express' clients. Practically every girl in the business felt the same.

The truth is that every minute of a prostitute's working hours is precious. Sex workers abhor sitting on a client's lap and making conversation. A man may derive pleasure out of necking and kissing, but the girl in his arms is always acting. The man also believes that he is sexually arousing the girl to squeeze maximum pleasure out of her in bed. The fact is that she is as cold as a piece of meat in a refrigerator. She plays along to fuel his excitement only so that she has less work to do in bed. A prostitute's face never betrays her feelings. Even regulars with years of brothel experience under their belt, so to speak, are deceived by such performances. Having been a prostitute, I never had to enrol myself in a film institute or a theatre academy to learn acting. For prostitutes, acting is not a hobby, it is a survival skill.

I entered the cabin with my client and shut the door. He sat on the edge of the cot with his legs dangling, waiting for me.

He was completely unknown to me. I was looking at his face for the first time.

He seemed to be around thirty years old, slightly built. His long face looked like a stretched rubber band. His cheekbones were high and appeared even more prominent under the light of the bulb. He had thin lips, a sharp nose and mischievous brown eyes. He wore a white kurta with chikan embroidery and old-fashioned drawstring pyjamas. He looked like a small-time crook, probably a member of a gang of pickpockets or someone who peddled movie tickets in black.

Hanging my miniskirt and T-shirt on the wall, I asked, 'What's your name?'

He did not reply.

He was absorbed in the task of untying the drawstring. The knot, like an enemy from a previous birth, was giving him a tough time.

I asked again, 'What do you do for a living?'

'I untie drawstrings!' he joked drily without looking up.

I knelt before him in my bra and panty to help him undress. He straightened up slowly. Loosening the knot, I teased, 'Still haven't learned how to untie a drawstring?'

I paid dearly for mocking his masculine pride. I hadn't expected this wiry client to hold fort for more than five minutes. He rammed me for thirty minutes straight. Every bone in my body rattled like old parts of a broken jalopy. The skinny bastard hammered me so savagely that I felt I would lose consciousness. Still, I did not allow any reaction to show on my face, lest he felt I was defeated. He got off the bed and strutted to the mori. I was forced to get up; my job wasn't done yet. As he squatted near the bucket, I washed his penis with Dettol water. Then I washed myself and stood up.

Normally, clients tip a girl a rupee or two before leaving. If they forget, the girls don't hesitate to remind them. Some greedy girls attach themselves limpet-like to clients to extract a tip, like beggars who chase people on every other street corner of Bombay.

I never asked for a tip. It was the client's prerogative to express gratitude. Though I did not hold out my hand for baksheesh, the tapori tipped me generously. Not in cash, but in the form of movie tickets! From his kurta pocket, he extracted a wad of tickets. He took out four from the top and put them in my palm. I thanked him. Humming a song, he walked out with a broad grin stretched across his face.

I collapsed on the bed. I badly needed some rest. All alone in the cabin, I felt like my body had been pummelled by a heavyweight boxer. Every limb was crying out in pain. I had serviced countless men over the years. Even after a ferocious ape like Babu Rao had done all he could, I had stood tall. But this mosquito had knocked me out. For a few minutes, I lay unmoving. I had not even worn my clothes. I was in my bra and underwear, lying face-down on the bed with my arms spread out. Crushed.

For no particular reason my eyes settled on a portrait of Indira Gandhi, hanging on the opposite wall. As I lay there, I scanned my memory to remember whose photos were hung in the other cabins. If I recalled correctly, the cabin to my right had a photograph of Morarji Desai and the one to the left had Lal Bahadur Shastri's. As I continued to wrack my brain, I also remembered that the walls of Sakhu Bai's cages had been decorated with framed pictures of gods and goddesses. The warehouse, on the other hand, was adorned with photographs of national leaders. Only Gangu Bai knew the reason behind this strange choice.

Suddenly, the door of the cabin opened and Julie entered with a client. She stopped in her tracks, surprised to see my half-naked body spread-eagled on the bed.

'Are you all right?' she asked as she walked up to me.

Her client was still at the door.

I sat up. While I dressed, I mustered the energy to respond. 'I think I may have to take a break . . . maybe for a week,' I said haltingly. 'My body has been aching since afternoon.'

I had no desire to return to my room. I really did need to buy a painkiller for my sore body. I stepped out of the brothel. It was around nine. The fourteen streets were already swirling with life. The infamous red lights of the district were turned on—though in reality some were green and blue and pink as well, depending on the brothel owner. The lanes were teeming with raucous street vendors eager to catch the attention of randy Romeos who were busy eyeing wares of a different sort. The impatient honks of taxis and the clip-clop of the Victoria horses trying to mend their way through this tumult added to the gaiety. I glanced affectionately at the gangs of girls trying their luck on the pavement, as I had once done.

I went to the paan-beedi shop and got two paans packed. As I strolled aimlessly, I realized I was close to the liquor joint where Sattar worked. My heart started beating faster. I was curious to see him at his new workplace.

I set off at a brisk pace. To reach the liquor den, one had to pass through an unnamed alley that smelt of cheap spirits and was squeezed between two houses. The entrance to the alley was concealed behind a fraying chatai. Outside sat a gruff gorilla of a man who wore only a brown lungi and a grimy skullcap. He scowled at my figure-hugging T-shirt which said 'WOW' and raised the mat to let me pass.

Hesitantly, I stepped into the lane. I was surprised to see that the pathway to the joint was clean. To reach the serving area, I had to go downstairs to the basement. There, two soiled wooden benches, along with unsteady chairs and lopsided tables, were packed tightly in the limited space. The men resting their elbows on the tables were busy drinking, chatting and cursing loudly. I tried looking for Sattar, but it was difficult to see through the fog of tobacco smoke.

I was still at the door when, along with Sattar, all the drunkards turned their heads one after another to stare at me. An unexpected hush fell across the basement. Forty-eight pairs of eyes were on me. Seeing an attractive woman in their male bastion, they were first shocked, then ecstatic. Someone whistled lustily. A couple of drunkards staggered up from their chairs and offered me a drink. A sozzled truck driver, at least three pegs down, jumped up on the bench with his glass and gyrated his hips, imploring me to dance with him. Another swarthy fellow boldly came forward, held me in his arms, and squeezed me tightly. He wanted me to sit on his lap. I panicked. I tried to wriggle out of his hairy arms, but he was too strong for me. As he smooched me awkwardly, I was pricked by his stubble, which was so bristly that you could scrub dirty dishes with it. Sattar rushed to my rescue. He punched the drunkard on his face till his nose started bleeding.

I stared at Sattar in surprise. My naïve illusion had been shattered. Sattar was no longer my sweet boyish companion. He was a man, and a tough one at that!

Of course, he still hadn't figured out why I had come to his liquor den. Actually, I too didn't have any good reason to be there . . . or perhaps I did. I took out a movie ticket from my pocket and placed it in his palm. His eyes kept surveying my face. My heart was thudding against my chest walls. The way he looked at me, I felt shy. I felt beautiful. I could swear I almost felt unsoiled. Before my face betrayed my crazy emotions, I turned and strode back out to the real world.

8

Everyone was going gaga over the film *Amar Akbar Anthony* those days. It had been running houseful at the Royal Opera House theatre for three weeks, with box seats still being sold in black for as much as Rs 25 to Rs 30. My tapori client had tipped me four tickets for this film.

I had decided to wear a silk *gharaara* with a matching pink dupatta and a low-necked blouse that teased the gentle swell of my breasts. On a whim, I tied my hair up in a ponytail, like an adolescent schoolgirl. Sattar and I were in the reserved box seats. He seemed to be tense sitting close to me for the first time and constantly crossed and uncrossed his legs. And if his legs were still, he would shift his weight from left to right.

The Royal Opera House was one of the old heritage cinemas that had special boxes in the auditorium to offer privacy to wealthy couples and families. These boxes usually had four or eight seats. Our box had four, two of which we had occupied. The remaining two were empty. I had the tickets for these seats as well, but instead of selling them I had torn them into pieces.

After a mandatory short film by the Films Division of India played out, the feature film started. I glanced behind to confirm if the other two seats were still empty. They were. I was pleased. If there was any difference between this family box and the plywood cubicle at the brothel, it was only that there was one wall missing here. Not that it mattered—it was so dark that no one could see us.

I stretched my right arm carefully behind the seat and rested it on Sattar's shoulders. This was enough to turn him on. As if I had lightly dragged a feather across the length of his body, a shiver ran through him, from his feet to his head.

I had anticipated this. It was Sattar's turn to make a move now. He hesitantly extended his left hand and placed it lightly on my thigh. What happened next was unexpected! I felt a tremor within me, like a girl who had just turned sixteen. I felt my nipples rise and a warm flush spreading across my chest. My breath was caught in my lower abdomen and my muscles began craving for more of his strong yet gentle touch.

A few minutes later, I heard the squeaking of the chair as he adjusted himself. My heart leapt. He turned and cupped my face in his hands. The ferocity with which he kissed my lips ignited my whole body.

Until then, I had been deluded into believing that having being with countless men over the years had deadened my body, killed every tender emotion and numbed all romantic feeling. How wrong I had been!

One touch from Sattar seemed to have turned me into a virgin. Sattar was my first . . .

After a few seconds, I forgot that I was a prostitute. That fingerprints of innumerable men were imprinted on my skin. And that not a single inch of my body had been left untouched. I felt as if my body was like that of a girl's in a bridal sari.

I blossomed. A hundred thousand jasmine buds opened their petals in my chest and spread their fragrance to the farthest corners of my body. My heart drummed at an abnormal speed. In the darkness, I could hear it knocking clearly; threatening to explode out of my breasts. A single touch of Sattar's lips had set off all these fireworks.

After the film ended, a little before six, I looked at Sattar. He had to reach the liquor joint by seven. I too had to get to work at Gangu Bai's. But neither of us was in the mood to work. We walked from the Opera House to Chowpatty and bought two kulfis. Enjoying them, we went to Marine Drive and found a bench that overlooked the sea.

It was sunset time. Above the horizon, the sky was changing colours. Half the orange disc of the sun had already disappeared into the sea. We watched silhouettes of birds sweeping across the sky, flying back to their nests and little ones. We sat, lost in our thoughts, watching the heavenly drama in technicolour.

'Kumud?' Sattar finally broke the silence. I turned to look at him, but he had fallen silent again. It felt like he wanted to say something but was struggling to find the right words. 'Kumud . . .' he started again and then abruptly added, 'If I don't report for work, Dawood Bhai will be upset.'

I understood that Sattar had intended to say one thing but had ended up saying something else.

'But . . .' I took the conversation forward. 'Dawood is in the lockup, isn't he?'

'He was released yesterday.'

'Come,' I said, as I stood up from the bench, 'there is still time. You get back to your job and I will go back to my warehouse.'

He too stood up, but his legs, instead of taking him towards Kamathipura, started walking towards Nariman Point. His love for me was pulling him in one direction and his fear of Dawood Khan in the other.

I slipped my fingers into his. He clutched my hand like it was a lifeline and looked into my eyes. The golden glow the sun had left behind illuminated the contours of our faces. We wandered around for hours, hand in hand, caressed by the ocean breeze. The ends of my pink dupatta danced in our wake.

We reached Kamathipura around eleven. Sattar wanted to spend the rest of the night with me. Instead of going back to the warehouse, I approached the old whore who rented her bug-free shack to streetwalkers. In the old days, I would have paid one rupee for fifteen minutes. Today, I handed the woman Rs 75 and booked the shack for the whole night. I wanted Sattar to not only experience the peaks of ecstasy in a woman's body, but to also become familiar with the enduring warmth of a lover's arms.

I spent the whole night there with Sattar.

It was an exhilarating, unforgettable night. After the first sweet spasm of love, we lay in each other's arms, lost in long, deep kisses, his hands cupping my breasts. We clung to each other like two spirits who could not be separated. His hunger for me remained undiminished through the night. He kissed me like he wanted to consume me entirely—a guppy wanting to devour a wild fish. And then—slowly, rhythmically, gently—he would begin moving down my body again . . . and I would seem to rise again.

When dawn broke, we were lying on the bed naked, exhausted and satiated. I glowed as if this had been my wedding night, as if I had gifted all that I had inside me to Sattar. For the first time, I felt that I was spoken for, that I belonged to someone. Sattar had not only conquered my body, he had planted his flag in my soul.

Even bodybuilders and macho gangsters, in my experience, failed to leave a mark on their first try. But Sattar was different. He showed no sign of nervousness. Perhaps the difference was love. Where there is love, there is no failure. Love magnetically draws us towards the summits of success.

In less than two months, Aai's undernourished body had filled out and it became hard to see her bones. When she had arrived in Bombay, you could count her ribs. Her shrivelled breasts were now full, like those of a pregnant woman. And there was a reason for it.

Aai wasn't that old. The age difference between us was only around twenty years. If I was twenty-two, Aai must have been in her early forties. It was just that she had known too little shade and faced too much of the scorching sun.

Its blistering heat had sucked the life out of her and dried her up like a twig; hunger and worry had gnawed at her crumbling body.

After the drought, she had begun to look as if she was on the wrong side of fifty. Had she not come to Bombay, her health would not have improved as rapidly. Now, a glance at her was enough to tell her real age—one might even guess a year or two younger!

'Aai,' I teased her, 'if you wish, I can ask Gangu Bai to settle you here.'

'And what will I do here?'

'What you taught me in Tulu. I'm certain you will attract at least half a dozen clients a day.'

A blush spread across her cheeks. The thought pleased her. Yet, with a wave of her hand, she declined my offer. Aai had a strong attachment to village life. After it rained, the black tar roads of Bombay did not explode with fragrance like the red earth back home. Where would she find the transparent blue village sky in the city's grey canopy, which looked as solid as an unwashed glass roof?

There was another reason why she wouldn't stay in Bombay. During the drought, she had taken in Kumkum, Constable Naik's almond-eyed daughter. Aai had left the house in her charge when she came to Bombay. The girl hadn't grown up yet, but Aai had pinned her hopes upon her: she was certain that once the girl came of age, men of all ages would line up for her. Aai wanted to spend the rest of her life in the village with Kumkum. Though this made me sad, I did not insist.

Aai's stuff needed to be packed. When she had come to Bombay, she had brought along only one bruised tin trunk that had been stuffed to bursting point. I had bought her a dozen new saris. It took some Herculean effort to be able to fit all the new saris into the old trunk. In the corners, I jammed some small, useful gifts I had purchased for Kumkum: fake jewellery, a fancy comb, lipstick, a box of powder and a perfume. In addition, I gave Aai a basket of mangoes to take back home.

Aai was about to leave when Gangu Bai dropped in, her trademark cigarette between her lips. All the days that Aai had been here, Gangu Bai hadn't spoken a single word to her. She hadn't even bothered to cast her regal glance upon Aai. Given this, I was surprised to see her sudden entry and the warmth of her radiant smile.

Behind her, Devi followed with a tray bearing gifts: a box of Mahim Halwa sweets and a dazzling nine-yard silk sari. She offered us a heartfelt apology for not having found the time to meet Aai earlier. 'I hope you didn't have any problem during your stay here?' she asked finally.

She was such a gracious hostess that not only Aai, but even I was deeply touched. Aai touched her feet. 'After all you have done for us, sister, please . . . don't embarrass us further. Your place is heaven on earth. Seeing my daughter joyful here, my old wilted heart has blossomed again.'

'Next time you visit your darling, you won't recognize her,' Gangu Bai said, taking a drag from her cigarette. 'She was not made to slog with the crowd here. I have arranged for an air-conditioned bungalow for her. Hopefully, by next month, she will move to her new home.'

My eyes widened with surprise. I couldn't believe that my life would so unexpectedly take such a grand turn! So far, besides Sattar, I had disclosed this ambition only to Bhagwan Das, the top dalal of Bombay's red-light areas. I had even hinted to him that I would be open to offering him an envelope stuffed with hundred-rupee notes in return for his services. Other than these people, no one knew of my secret desire. Gangu Bai had read my heart.

That day, I realized there was really no word in any language that could express what I felt for Gangu Bai. She was more than a mother. She was the divine overseer of life and the orchestrator of destiny in these fourteen godless lanes. Aai, in her own way, had expressed the same feeling—she had bowed in supplication with folded hands as she backed away, thanking Gangu Bai. Two silent tears of gratitude had rolled down her face.

I dropped Aai off at Victoria Terminus. When her train arrived, I helped her find her seat and then stood on the platform, next to the window of her compartment, holding her hand until the train rolled into motion with a jolt. As it moved away from the station, I felt my cheeks wet.

When I returned to the boisterous streets of Kamathipura that night, my life felt empty—a bottomless pit. But while Aai's absence was tormenting me, my air-conditioned palace was tugging me forward. Swinging like a pendulum between hope and grief, I stepped into the hall. The girls surrounded me—cheering, laughing and congratulating. The shower of compliments temporarily washed off the sorrow of separation.

Of course, these hard-boiled girls had their own catty way of complimenting me.

'Oye! From now on, Kumud will only let a wealthy saand mount her!'

'God has blessed her with a lucky cunt! How else can any girl's rate shoot up from Rs 22 to Rs 50 in such a short time.'

'She's really mastered her job!'

Someone else in the crowd asked, 'What about us, eh?'

' . . . still know only blow jobs.'

The girls cracked up into peals of laughter. Behind the cheers of camaraderie, I could sense the envy in their voices. I did not feel bad. I knew them well. They were common hookers who cursed the job and hated their clients. They possessed neither ambition nor self-discipline. The bloom of youth, which they vainly peddled to anyone and everyone, was as transient as a fading flower. In those lanes, I had seen twenty-year-old hags.

At 2 a.m., when the liquor joint shuttered for the night, Sattar would come to me. His arrival time was fixed. I would make sure to take care of all my clients by then and wait for him in my room.

Till the previous night, I had been sharing the guest room with Aai. Because of Sattar, I needed privacy. So I had pulled a temporary curtain in the middle of the room; on one side Aai would lie snoring and on the other Sattar and I would lie entwined in slippery tenderness. But tonight was special. I had the whole room at my disposal.

I gleefully pulled down the curtain and went for a bath. I powdered my armpits, neck and breasts. Of course, I did this every day for the job, but to welcome Sattar I touched up my face again, wore a clean dress and tucked in the wrinkled, half-unravelled bedsheet so that no creases showed.

I had bought a box of incense sticks too. I lit one and placed it in the incense stand in the corner. I stopped for a moment to inhale the sweet smell of the rose-scented agarbattis. I did not know if every woman in love took such pains, but for me this had become my nightly ritual for the past month.

It was half past two. The incense stick had turned to limp ashes, but Sattar hadn't come yet. I was a little worried. How come Sattar, who rushed to be with me on the dot every night, was late? Before I made myself sick with worry, I diverted my thoughts. How far would Aai's train have reached? Would she have got any sleep on the upper berth? I thought about her for a few minutes before focusing on my soon-to-be home.

Where was this air-conditioned bungalow? Who owned it? As far as I knew, Gangu Bai didn't own any. Rehmat Khan Lala had three. Was that where Gangu Bai planned to send me? I didn't know for sure, but one thing I was certainly happy about—Babu Rao was not in this business.

Before the clock touched three, the door to my room burst open. Startled, I sat up on my bed. Sattar's silhouette was framed in the doorway.

He was wearing a dark jacket over a striped red shirt and a lungi that came down to his toes. Around his neck was a scarf with a film star's face printed on it. His hair was dishevelled.

What had come over this boy who padded to my room every night like a playful puppy wanting to snuggle? He stumbled unevenly towards me and I got my answer.

He was drunk! I was flustered: I hated alcoholics. Despite every provocation and pressure, I hadn't allowed a drop of liquor into my body. Even if a client tried to bully me into having a peg, I nudged it away politely with a smile. I did not mind if a client wanted me to serve him liquor. Even if he wanted me to hold the glass to his lips and offer him sips, I gladly played along. It was part of my job. But I could not accept my own lover coming to bed in that obnoxious state.

I kept mum: nagging a drunkard is as futile as trying to reason with him. Sattar looked like he was possessed by a demonic spirit from the netherworld. He staggered beside me on the bed and forced his hand into my blouse. He knew that was where I kept my money. His demands had been increasing over the last week, so I had stopped keeping notes inside my blouse.

He pushed his hand deeper. When it came out empty, he arched his eyebrows in surprise. Then he pulled me by my hair and raged, 'Where is the money?'

'I was on leave today.'

He repeated his question with more force, 'WHERE IS THE MONEY!'

I repeated my answer and tried to calm him down. 'Sattar, you have come drunk today. Please . . .'

Whack! He slapped me hard across the face. I was speechless. Sattar, my boyish companion who had become my adoring lover, was progressing at supersonic speed. He had long been hooked on to gambling, but today he had embraced one more vice—liquor.

A wave of disgust swept over me, yet there was little I could do. He was the only man for whom I was willing to endure every thrashing, every humiliation. *Why?* Sattar had made me a complete woman. He was the only man with whom I found total satisfaction. When he entered me, the fatigue of the night would melt away. I could not live without him.

He slapped me again, twice. I clung to him tighter.

Sattar! Sattar! Sattar!

I hugged him and began sobbing. He began raining blows on my back. But I did not let go. I was once again amazed at my body's capacity to endure pain.

My dear reader, do you pity me? Don't. The ferocity soon turned into furious caressing and frantic kissing. I was aroused by his passion. I wanted this pleasure to continue for as long as possible, to take us both beyond all limits. I kissed him, bit his earlobe and stroked his manhood until he mounted me in frenzied excitement.

We were one again. I felt myself floating.

He began thrusting madly, like a bull in heat. I moaned and writhed, but he didn't stop. He took this as a test of his masculinity and began heaving, red and furious in the face, with renewed power, driving himself deeper as my breaths became shorter. And then I screamed as ecstasy flooded my pores and exploded into an orgasm that hundreds of men before him had failed to give me.

My dear reader, do you still pity me? Then you haven't experienced love the way I have. It was the first time I'd ever felt this way about anyone, and I was ready to give him anything. Even if that meant exploring the animal depth inside us. You've walked only in that fenced-off little society garden—you have yet to explore the jungle. Whatever your moral science teachers taught you, the truth is that sex and violence have always been deeply intertwined within us. That night, our lovemaking took us to a peak we had not touched before. As I lay on the bed, I felt as if I would die of pleasure. How long would there be newer peaks of passion to conquer? I did not know; and that night, I did not care.

9

I had spent the entire week grappling with a dilemma. It was peculiar: Gangu Bai had released me from her warehouse to work in a posh, new air-conditioned bungalow-brothel to be inaugurated soon. This was exhilarating news. My wildest dream was coming true!

And then I found out that the air-conditioned bungalow was owned by Babu Rao. The bright rush of happiness that had been coursing through me was contaminated by a dark stream of distress.

In the past four years, Babu Rao had opened nine opium joints in Kamathipura. The income that these dens guaranteed him, coupled with the money coming in from smuggling, had ensured he was wealthy. This year, he had decided to expand his business by venturing into the flesh trade: he was soon to be the proud owner of high-class brothels as well.

Actually, this was the shortest route to making more money. Here, in Kamathipura, several taporis had begun by putting up a girl—lured, forced or bought—into this business. Then, with the earnings from that one girl, the goons purchased more girls and expanded their operation.

Babu Rao had bought fifteen girls, including me. According to Gangu Bai, he had paid between Rs 3000 and Rs 5000 for each girl—each of whom he had personally chosen from different brothels. But my deal had cost him more because, sensing his desperation, Gangu Bai had managed to squeeze Rs 8000 out of him.

After taking her 25 per cent commission, Gangu Bai, with all honesty, handed me my share of Rs 6000. I could scarcely believe my eyes. Though there wasn't a single image of any deity in the warehouse, I was certain that Yellamma was indeed there. Had Gangu Bai been crafty like Sakhu Bai, she would not have given me a single paisa, and I would never have found out about the deal.

Finally, I made up my mind. Money had changed hands. Gangu Bai had been fair to me. Babu Rao had paid top-shelf price for me. It was too late to back out. More importantly, Gangu Bai had given her word. And her word was more valuable than currency. I had no option but to move to the air-conditioned bungalow. I left the warehouse quietly, with some trepidation. Churning with anticipation, I hesitantly stepped into my new abode. And I was dazzled.

Like Gangu Bai's warehouse, this place was single-storeyed too. The ground floor housed a Chinese restaurant and two shops; the first floor was where we stayed. To visit us, one had to pass through a lane called 'Bachu ki Baadi' and then climb a dozen squeaky steps that sang a new tune every time.

Bachu Ki Baadi was famous for its seekh kebabs. Every night, food lovers from all over the city would drive down to this place. Together with kebabs, one could also partake of the pleasures of *shabab* if they wished. The lane echoed with courtesans, as it did with history. It was said that legendary singer Begum Akhtar once sang here and Saadat Hasan Manto, the writer, visited frequently too.

At the foot of the stairs, Babu Rao had posted his trusted henchman, Kallu Mamad—made more of concrete than flesh—as the bouncer. Walking past him, one had to climb up the flight of creaky stairs that led to the door of the reception hall. I walked in to have a cool brush from an air conditioner sweep across my face. A crystal chandelier tinkled as it swayed gently overhead.

The hall was not even half the size of Gangu Bai's warehouse. Yet, it was spacious enough to comfortably host a hundred guests in one night. The floors were carpeted from end to end. Plump new sofas stood against three of the walls, interrupted by discreet side tables. Ashtrays were placed neatly at the centre of each table. In one corner, a large television was set within a carved wooden stand. As I stood admiring the tableau, a middle-aged matron popped up and stood before me.

'Name?'

I told her.

'From Maa's warehouse?'

I nodded.

'My name is Salma . . . Salma Bi, if you wish to address me respectfully. I'm the caretaker. Come, let me show you your room.'

I followed her in silence. My luggage consisted of just one suitcase that had been newly purchased to make a good impression and fit in with the posh decor. We walked through a door at the far end of the hall and found ourselves in a corridor. There were cubicles on both sides. The cabins to the right were for entertaining clients and those to the left were our living quarters. Each room was shared by two girls.

Salma Bi led me to the third room on the left, and my eyes lit up once again. How perfectly pretty it was! It had two divans that doubled up as beds, with two elegantly carved wooden cupboards on either side. A common bathroom was concealed behind a Kashmiri woodwork partition.

'Meet Kanchan Bala,' Salma Bi said, introducing me to my roommate who had arrived early and settled herself. 'She has come from Number 207.'

The caretaker then spoke a few words, formally introducing me to Kanchan Bala. We smiled cordially at each other. And then Salma Bi left the room.

Kanchan Bala was a picturesque beauty, her smile was as perfect as the smiles that sold soaps and colas on billboards and newspapers. If my skin was honey, hers was milk. My crimson-flecked teeth had dulled, and I even had a gold tooth, but her teeth were a string of flawless pearls. Her body was compact. She had a little excess weight around her bottom, but I thought that only made her more desirable!

'Where are you from?' I asked, as I opened my suitcase on the divan.

'Punjab,' she said, without looking up. She was sitting on her divan with her legs stretched out, her back cushioned by two pillows against the wall. Her big brown eyes were gazing blankly into a film magazine.

'I am from Tulu, in Satara district,' I said, though she hadn't asked.

She nodded in vague acknowledgement without taking her eyes off the magazine.

'When did you come to Bombay?' I asked, arranging my clothes in the cupboard.

'It's been almost three years . . .' she said, looking up at last. A sigh betrayed that it wasn't a happy memory. After a brief pause, she asked, 'What about you?'

'Around the same.'

Kanchan Bala then put the magazine aside and suddenly changed the subject. 'Did you choose this profession or were you tricked into it?'

'It is our family business.'

'What! What do you mean?'

'My mother is also a prostitute. My grandma, in her heyday, was the pride of the Maratha court. She was the concubine of the Peshwa. A connoisseur of classical music and dance. In fact, she was a trained classical singer and Kathak dancer.'

Kanchan Bala stared at me with doleful eyes. After I finished arranging my clothes and belongings, I sat cross-legged on my divan, facing her. 'You know my history. Now it's your turn.'

'I would, if I had anything to say.'

Seeing her hesitation, I coaxed her, 'Come on now, everyone has a story to tell.'

'My father is one of the richest farmers in Punjab. I eloped with my boyfriend to come to Bombay. That bhadwa sold me to a broker and disappeared. He also stole my jewellery worth Rs 10,000 and Rs 5000 in cash.'

I was saddened but not shocked. Sewers in the red-light area overflowed with similar tales of betrayal and heartbreak, abandonment and abuse. I expressed sincere empathy and asked, 'How do you feel now?'

'Like a sparrow fluttering uselessly inside a golden cage. I would fly away if I could.'

'The doors are open. Fly away!'

'Once you step into this profession, all other doors are shut forever.'

Before she could elaborate, Salma Bi walked into our room once again. 'There is a mahurat ceremony at six,' she said, addressing both of us. 'Be there on time.'

It was two in the afternoon. We hadn't had lunch yet. We were to eat at the Chinese restaurant downstairs. At least for that day, food was on the house. We were to make our own arrangements from the next day.

Within an hour, we were back in our room. It would be a long night, we knew, so we decided to use the time to take a short nap. Around five, my eyes opened to muffled, happy sounds of the mahurat arrangements: echoes of instructions (and abuses) being barked, tinkling of cutlery being arranged, the drone of the air conditioner on full to cool the room before the VIPs and other *bade mehmaan* arrived.

We quickly splashed some water on ourselves and changed into fresh clothes. I wore my favourite baby pink sari with a matching blouse that clung to every curve of my breasts. Kanchan Bala chose a long peach-coloured kaftan that had tantalizing side slits leading up to her waist.

We reached the hall around quarter to six. The guests had already begun to arrive. Babu Rao had invited only important contacts and personal friends to enjoy at his expense. This meant that they could sample the services of any girl for free before the brothel was officially declared open. He had ensured that the number of men on the guest list did not exceed that of the girls, so that each man could enjoy at least one girl as long as he wanted. Beyond this, there were two VVIP guests who were also expected—Gangu Bai and Rehmat Khan Lala.

The sounds of a shehnai wafted in like fragrance amongst the guests. The chandelier looked festive with confetti balloons and colourful streamers swirling below it. The walls were dotted with shimmering paper stars and silver moons. The atmosphere was truly celebratory. In all my years in this profession, I had never witnessed the inauguration of a brothel before.

By 6.15 p.m., with the growing commotion caused by the new arrivals, the wailing of the shehnai became irrelevant. The hall came alive with the prattle of girls and the chatter of guests. Salma Bi had given us clear instructions: we were to lavish all our charms on the invitees. It was our job to ensure that no one left unsatisfied.

Sharp at 6.30 p.m., Babu Rao walked in with two pandits and the ceremony commenced, quite like the pooja that flags off a Bollywood film shoot. In practised unison, the pandits recited Sanskrit mantras and shlokas to invoke divine favour for Babu Rao's earthly venture.

The breaking of the ceremonial coconut signalled the end of the ritual. Babu Rao's friends reached out to congratulate him—hugging, pumping his hands vigorously, slapping his back and showering praise on him. Rehmat Khan Lala

hugged him thrice—in keeping with the Pathan tradition—
as if they were chieftains of two tribes.

As I watched this scene unfold, the girls paired off with
the male guests. I realized that all the dignitaries were taken
while I stood rooted to the spot like a dummy. There was no
one left. No, wait . . . there was one man left—Babu Rao.

The pandits, knowing that what was about to happen
there would not win divine favour, slinked away. The
party began. Waiters from the Chinese restaurant spread
out across the room carrying bottles of beer and tall glasses.
After escorting Rehmat Khan Lala and Gangu Bai to the
door, Babu Rao came up to me with a big grin. 'Do you
like this place?'

I nodded. He guided me towards an unoccupied sofa and
sat down. I had no choice but to sit next to him.

'Kumud,' he spoke seriously, as he opened a bottle of beer
and poured out two glasses. 'I respect you. A hundred whores
of Kamathipura are no match for you. Proud. Principled.
Disciplined. The rest are just regular *randis*.'

I was flattered. Babu Rao seemed to be speaking from the
heart. His expression was crude but the emotion was 100 per
cent pure.

He offered me a glass of beer.

'I don't drink,' I said with a polite smile.

He was silent for a second and then looked at me
incredulously, as if he couldn't quite believe what I had told
him. After a few seconds, he asked, 'Really?'

I smiled again.

'But this is just beer.'

'I like to keep my body clear of all intoxicating things.'

His face clouded over as if he was trying to hold my words in his head, so that he could think about them later maybe. His brain proved unequal to the task. He just glanced at me twice before putting the glass to his lips and draining its contents.

'Your wish,' he muttered. In the next instant, he had emptied my glass too and caught every last drop on his extended tongue. The bloody clown was downing beer as if it was water. Two glasses down, Babu Rao's eyes began to get the familiar glassy twinkle. Putting an arm around me, he changed the subject.

'Kumud! Do you know who these guests are?'

I did not.

He told me about each of the men present in the hall. My eyes widened. His guests included a big-name film producer, a Parsi cinema-owner, a reputed builder, a five-star hotel manager, a CBI officer and even the personal assistant of a national politician.

It was evident from the assortment of men assembled there that Babu Rao was stealthily trying to extend his domain. He was cautiously stepping into the league where he had Gangu Bai and Rehmat Khan Lala as competitors. It was a different thing that Gangu Bai was still way ahead of both men—the power she wielded in Kamathipura was unmatched.

Rehmat Khan Lala came a close second. But there was a vast difference between the way Gangu Bai and Lala wielded power. What Gangu Bai accomplished with a smile, he needed an army of foot soldiers to achieve. Of course, his own raw strength formed the base of his power. He was such a terror that even senior cops didn't dare to cross him. On top of that, he also had the power of money on his side.

When Lala's son, Dawood, was arrested for the murder of Bhajan Lal, Babu Rao had done everything to ensure he remained behind bars. Yet Dawood was cleared of all charges and released.

Though the final outcome had not been in Babu Rao's favour, he had established that he was someone to reckon with. In the future, he would not be bullied by Lala—he would strike back with confidence. He was expanding his influence as fast as he could to contend with an adversary like Lala.

After spending half an hour with me, Babu Rao wandered away to attend to his guests. Before all the beer was drained, the waiters brought in whisky and rum bottles: it was time for hard liquor. Plates piled high with salted snacks, prawns and chicken lollipops continued to circulate. Babu Rao, who had chosen his guests carefully, took time out to chat with each one.

I stood up from the sofa and started attending to the guests. With my best smile, I held out plates of salted pistachios and almonds, and engaged them in conversation. Babu Rao noticed from the corner of his eyes. He looked pleased and proud.

In the next round, I offered the guests a platter of seekh kebabs. One of them, whom Babu Rao had introduced as the producer, took the platter from my hands and set it aside. Holding me by the wrist, he pulled me on to his lap.

There was already a Nepali girl in a transparent turquoise blouse sitting beside him. She was cute, but she was a novice, probably recently brought in from across the border. She couldn't understand Hindi, which was probably why Mr Producer was getting bored.

I realized that a girl's body alone did not suffice. If that was true, the producer would have been perfectly satisfied with the petite girl in his arms—she was as pretty as a doll, with perfect breasts and pink-tipped nipples poking through the transparent fabric. Without a word, the girl got up and melted into the crowd. I took her place.

'What's your name?' the fat-cheeked producer asked me, as he took a sip of the whisky. The tiny fingers of his free hand were feeling up my back. I was sitting on his lap—or rather, trying to sit, because his balloon-like belly left very little space for me to perch on comfortably.

'A prostitute doesn't have a name!' I answered. 'Call her by any name you desire. She can be whatever name fuels your fantasies.'

My reply seemed to amuse him. 'Yet they are called by one particular name, aren't they?'

'Almost all prostitutes have more than one name. One name a prostitute shares with her clients. Her friends know her by a different name. The third is her real name. That name has the fragrance of the native soil of her childhood—and that name has nothing to do with the many fake ones she adopts for the profession.'

The producer blinked his beady eyes.

I continued with a mischievous smile, 'This is also true of the heroines in your movies, isn't it?'

He put his empty glass on the table and agreed with me. 'I like the way you talk . . . interesting.' And then smiling for the first time, he asked, 'So tell me, by which name would you like me to call you?'

'Kumud.'

'No . . .' he asserted. 'I shall call you Cuckoo. I could listen to you for hours.'

The producer refilled his empty glass. By 11 p.m., he had had so much to drink that he was rendered wholly useless as a man. Even without the damping influence of alcohol, I doubt if he could have performed sexually; he was a hernia patient.

By 2 a.m., a hush had descended on our elite den. When the clock had struck one, most of the guests had already passed out and lost all sense of time and place. Some had crumbled on the sofas, others were sprawled out on the carpet. Those who had managed to take a girl into a cabin had collapsed inside, while a few had fallen just outside the cabins. Three men lay in the narrow corridor, like coiled snakes. Babu Rao had them all picked up and dropped to their residences.

I lay down in my room, on my bed. On the other one, Kanchan Bala was snoring like a motorcar idling. As I switched off the lights, my thoughts flew to Sattar. It was a little past 2 a.m., his fixed hour to knock on the door of our love nest at Gangu Bai's warehouse.

A few days before moving to the bungalow, I had given Sattar my new address. I knew he would no longer visit me as regularly. When our relationship had begun, he used to come every night between two and two-thirty. Then he got addicted to alcohol.

There were times when he had staggered in at three or four in the morning, drunk as a lord. On other nights, he had not showed up at all. When he did turn up, he robbed me of whatever money he could lay his hands on and vanished. He had become increasingly violent too. A fortnight before I left for Babu Rao's, he had thrashed me so savagely that I decided to kick him out for good.

The truth is that my determination hadn't lasted beyond a few hours. As the clock had inched towards 3 a.m., my rock-solid resolve to end the relationship had weakened and crumbled too. I had found myself longing for him. Finally, when he came that night, I had hugged him tightly and wept bitter tears.

After he had left, I had wondered what had come over a sensible girl like me. Why was I behaving like a doormat? Why was I so crazy about him? What magic did he possess that I felt incomplete without him? Who was he anyway? An ordinary street thug! Taporis like him could be found by the dozen in Kamathipura. He neither had any special ability, nor gentlemanly refinement. And yet . . . and yet . . . That was as far as my thoughts had taken me. For the questions that arose in my mind on lonely nights like those, I had no answers.

It was 3.30 a.m. I was restless. My yearning for Sattar began to grow into a physical craving. I wanted the weight of his body upon me, to feel the press of his chest against my bosom. I wanted to hold him and be held. I remembered the time we had watched *Amar Akbar Anthony* in the private box at the Opera House. He had only placed a palm on my thigh and I had trembled like a bride on her wedding night.

Sattar had his own way of appearing and disappearing, but I was certain that he would knock on my door soon, and we would again undress each other like cannibals hungry for sweet flesh.

Before I could think further, there was a soft, hesitant knock on the door. I jumped up from the divan. Consumed by fantasies of Sattar, my blood was racing and my heart palpitating. I eagerly unlocked the door and my body froze. In place of Sattar stood Babu Rao, drunk out of his thick skull.

10

Babu Rao was drunk on imported liquor. That night, Red Label Scotch—especially arranged in bulk from the docks—had been uncorked. Foreign liquor didn't stink like its desi counterpart, but my perceptive nose curled up in disgust all the same.

Seeing Babu Rao standing inebriated in front of me, my first instinct was to spit on his face. I was terrified too. Confused, I swung the door on his face. He had probably anticipated that I wouldn't submit without a struggle. Before the door banged shut, he wedged his foot in and flung it open. I stared at him blankly. He used this weak moment to spring on me like a panther.

Before I could utter a word, he pulled me by my hair and dragged me across the corridor into a vacant cabin. Slamming the door shut, he lifted me up and tossed me on the bed. Moaning in pain, I lay there quietly, awaiting the inevitable. Like a demon, Babu Rao towered over me, his eyes blazing fire. The man who had behaved like the perfect gentleman when he was sober had turned into Ravana under the effect of this accursed drink.

I quickly took stock of my situation. Why on earth was I resisting Babu Rao? If I wanted to continue in this air-conditioned bungalow, I did not have a choice. I would need to submit to every command without a whimper. To live inside a pond and antagonize the alligator would not be wise. Unfortunately, the resident alligator of my pond was also the owner—an ugly, square-jawed alligator with a pointy moustache and a discoloured birthmark under his right eye.

I pulled myself together. Brushing aside all thoughts of Sattar, I decided to put on my best performance. I sat up on the bed and smiled. He blinked in confusion. Taking advantage, I stood up and wrapped my arms around him.

He stood stiffly for a few seconds, doubt and caution playing on his face.

'Why do you hate me?' he asked.

'I don't . . .' I said, trying to think of an excuse.

'Why did you bang the door on my face?'

'You came at the wrong time . . . I was . . . expecting my man,' I blurted out and bit my tongue for making such a thoughtless blunder.

He sat on the bed next to me and sneered, 'Oh! That madarchod was your yaar?'

'Who? Did Sattar come here?'

He nodded, adding proudly, 'And from here, he must have gone straight to J.J. Hospital.'

I felt as if someone had crushed my heart under a heavy boot. For a few seconds, my mind refused to accept his words.

I forced myself to think, to reconstruct how the situation must have unfolded. Sattar must have come to visit me. Before he could have come up the stairs, he must have been stopped by that apartment-block of a man, Kallu Mamad. He must have tried to drunkenly challenge him, perhaps even landed a lucky punch or two. But then Kallu, perhaps with help from Babu Rao's other taporis, must have thrashed him badly. If any man from Rehmat Khan Lala's gang had the misfortune of being cornered by Babu Rao's toughies on their home turf, there was no way he would walk away with limbs intact. If Sattar wasn't already dead, he must be breathing his last.

I was seething with volcanic fury but was helpless. The howling within me was unbearable. But I could not allow it to explode yet. I swore to myself that I would make Babu Rao pay in blood for this. I thought to myself: I will make him curse the day he was born.

With supreme effort, I repressed my rage and resumed my performance. 'If I had any inkling that you minded it, I wouldn't have allowed him to enter this lane, Rao.'

'Well, whatever happened is for the best,' he said absently, lost in thoughts for a few seconds as he stroked my hair. 'I've been waiting for a long time for an opportunity to rough up one of Lala's men. Thanks to you, my lucky charm, I didn't have to do anything. The fly came right into the spider's web. Now that Lala knows that a real mard is standing in front of him.'

'If Lala is your enemy, why did you invite him to the inauguration?'

'That you won't understand,' he said. Then, with his pompous conviction that I wouldn't understand, he explained it to me. 'We pretend to be friends, but both of us know that there can only be one king in Kamathipura. He rules the streets today, but tomorrow will be my turn. Lala is haunted by this fear. Fucking petrified. He knows I have the *dum* to seize his throne. So he thrashes my men whenever he gets the opportunity.'

'And you, my dear Rao,' I said, my face registering appropriate awe to inflate his ego, 'you know how to pay him back . . . with interest.'

'If I don't, Lala's son will cut my head off like a Bakra Eid goat.'

I gave Babu Rao a night he would never forget. After every shot, he would sit on the chair facing the bed and gaze in wonder at my glistening naked body spread out on the sheets. To tease him, I would pull the covers up to my chin. He would pull it back down and a tug of war would follow, culminating in one more round.

He had probably never received such love even from his mistresses. I knew he had a mistress, lodged in a gifted apartment on posh Peddar Road. She had been living there for the past year and a half. She was a Christian girl, Ivy.

Babu Rao spent one night with her every week. What she did when he was not around was anyone's guess. But after this unforgettable night—five rounds in six hours—Babu Rao began to spend two to three nights with me every week. He even began to share his personal matters. When he was challenged by complex problems he could not wrap his thick brain around, he would consult me. Within a month, I had won his confidence.

The first month passed by in a flash. During the day, I would try to locate Sattar. I even disguised myself in a burkha to make a clandestine visit to his liquor den. Sattar was not there. I thought of going to the police, but I knew it would be of little use—if he had been a wealthy client, they would have at least tried, but Sattar was just a local tapori. I did manage to get his name added to their missing persons list, but his case was no more important for them than the hundreds of slippers stolen outside mosques and temples, which landed up in Chor Bazaar every day. So I continued on my own, scouring the streets with a vengeance. I refused to break down. That would mean accepting defeat, and that I could not do.

Amongst my circle, no one knew of Sattar's fate or his whereabouts. Rehmat Khan Lala's men knew everything. Yet they stonewalled every attempt to obtain information—as if they had been instructed to bury all trace of Sattar. This conspiracy of silence was not just distressing, it was baffling. *Was Sattar alive? Was he in a coma, a slowly rotting vegetable? Or had he died the same night that he was beaten?* I could not find a single clue.

As the days turned into weeks and then months, the restlessness in my heart only grew. Every night, it took me a long time to fall asleep. I would wake up exhausted, singed by memories. The only consolation was that I had no pressure on the work front. Babu Rao treated me like a queen. I could decide my work hours—and if I wanted to work at all. When I was not in the mood, I would lie on my divan all evening. Not even Salma Bi had the authority to disturb my peace.

Despite all these comforts, my wretchedness was deepening with every passing day. During the day, my mind would conjure up memories of the times Sattar would console me at the cages, when I thought I had no future. The time when he fought for me like a tiger at his liquor den. But the nights were worse.

At night, my thoughts would be flooded with sounds and sighs of lovemaking. Images of the moonlight outlining the muscles on his chest and shoulders as he drove deeper into my body. Even in total darkness, these memories glowed with unearthly illumination. I could not escape them. But I had to build a high wall around these thoughts so no one could glimpse, or even suspect, my secret grief. Least of all Babu Rao.

When Babu Rao visited me, I would wear elegant dresses with low V-shaped necklines because he loved the round tease of my honey-coloured breasts; the sweep of brown skin from my neck downwards beckoned him like an arrow, tantalizingly pointing his tired brain downwards to relief.

As soon as he would arrive, I would first measure out his Scotch and put the glass to his lips. With a radiant smile, I would fawn over him like a slave girl. The rest of the night, too, I would make sure my services were of the highest order.

My carefully chosen dress would be on the floor in minutes, crushed. For the next few hours, I would surrender to his perverted fantasies. Nothing was out of bounds. I knew what he—like every man—really wanted: a depraved whore with a childlike innocent smile. I would respond to his ardour with deep moans and sighs, and everything else I could, in order to make him believe that my lust for him equalled his own. Even as he left, I would hold out the friendly smile of a lapdog grateful to be petted by her master.

One evening, I noticed Kanchan Bala looking unusually pensive. I could see grey clouds of turmoil flitting across her face. A few days earlier, I had watched her listlessly turn the pages of a film magazine. I had asked her if she was upset. In response, she held up a smiling photo of Hema Malini and said glibly, 'I am upset because I am jealous of her.'

That day I realized that something was amiss in her life, but she did not want to share it with me. Perhaps she did not trust me enough to bare her heart. Before I could ask her more, she swung off the bed and left for the hall. It was time for business. Sitting alone in the room all day, I was getting bored as well. It had been two days since I had accepted a client. I walked to the hall to mingle with the girls and pass some time.

On the TV that stood in the corner, a Kuchipudi performance was in progress. Only one client was paying any attention to the dance. The rest of the girls were lounging around, gossiping and giggling. One impish client began fooling around. First, he pulled out a condom from his wallet and blew it up. Then he held it against the wall and popped it with his head. Was that a joke? No one laughed, but he got the attention he wanted. He asked the girls seriously, 'Where does a woman's honour lie?'

The girls were stumped. Then, one of them stepped forward and pulled up her choli so that her breasts spilled out. Jiggling them, she asked, 'Here?'

'Noooooooooo!' all the men shouted in unison. Someone whistled.

Another girl, facing us, spread her legs and lifted her lehenga up to her chin. 'Here?'

'Noooooooooo!' the men hoarsely chanted in chorus once again.

A third girl, who had been sitting silently in a corner, strutted to the centre of the room and displayed her naked bottom proudly. 'Here?'

This time, even the girls responded with raucous laughter.

I wasn't amused by bawdy humour, but I did recognize that even an elite air-conditioned gutter has its own stench. If you live here, you can't hold your breath forever.

There was a time, not long ago, when courtesans inspired awe and admiration. Society respected them. Kings and noblemen sent their sons to the courtesans' havelis to acquire social graces. These gifted women were not skilled merely in the art of lovemaking but were also well-versed in dance, music and literature. They were muses for great artists too; the uncredited inspiration behind many great works of art.

Such was the lineage to which I belonged. But in modern society, I did not enjoy the privileged position of my ancestors. Around the time of my grandmother's death, that culture was also buried six feet under. With it was buried the word 'courtesan'—else Aai would not be called a 'do damdi ki raand'.

People did not call me a slut to my face, but I knew that behind my back they tagged me with similar derogatory terms. I was not a common prostitute, but I wasn't very different either. I lived amidst them.

My rate may have shot up from Rs 2 to Rs 50, but my status in society remained the same. Whether I peddled my wares on the pavement, in a cage, in a warehouse or in a posh bungalow, the stigma remained the same. And my classification would remain the same: do damdi ki raand.

Was there no way I could pursue my calling as a courtesan and yet walk with pride amongst elite society? I still do not know why that thought crossed my mind that night. It was quickly followed by another question: What if I become an actress? If I could, that would solve my problem to a great extent. But before that, I had to extract my revenge on Babu Rao, and I had to avenge Sattar.

On television, the Kuchipudi dance recital had ended and the nightly 9 p.m. news bulletin had begun. But no one was paying attention. Constellated around their clients, the girls were chatting and roaring with laughter. Kanchan Bala was also part of that group, but her face was sombre, as if she was miles away. Suddenly, she rose from her chair and looked around. Spotting me, she walked directly up to me and asked if I wanted to have a paan with her. The unsteady tone of her voice asked me another question entirely. Together, we went downstairs to the paan shop.

'Kumud,' she whispered once we stepped on to the pavement. 'I want to confide in you.'

As we crossed the road, away from our den, I replied, 'Tell me.'

'I need to go to the doctor.'

'Why?'

'I caught an infection from some customer,' she explained in a shaky voice. 'There is blood in the urine. It burns . . . it's going to eat me up from the inside. I can't bear it. I can't tell anyone either.'

I contemplated her situation seriously. I hadn't faced this complication because I was always careful. I would insist on condoms—this ensured the client's safety as well as mine.

In rare cases, when the man was too drunk on alcohol—or on his powerful connections—and insisted on having a go without a condom, I would wash up thoroughly afterwards and get antibiotic shots without fail. I had also been fortunate that Gangu Bai always sided with her troops: if a client refused to wear armour, he could go elsewhere. Of course, from the other girls, I did know of venereal diseases: they were as old as the profession itself.

I ordered five paans at the shop, stuffed one into my mouth and requested Bhaiyaji to pack the remaining four. We turned and walked briskly towards the clinic of a Gujarati doctor a few hundred meters away. It was almost ten. I was not sure if the clinic would be open, but we decided to try our luck. When we got there a few minutes later, the doctor was in the process of switching off the lights. I hurried inside with Kanchan Bala.

The doctor, Pritamlal, was an elderly man, but had a tall, well-built frame that would put a youth to shame. To practise in a tough neighbourhood like Kamathipura—besides a medical degree—hard muscles sure would have come in handy. In a few minutes, I briefly explained the problem on Kanchan Bala's behalf. She sat with her head bowed, perspiring profusely. I was impressed that even at that odd hour, the doctor listened patiently. After noting everything I had said, he took Kanchan Bala behind a partition. The screened area was used for thorough physical examinations; the area outside, where I was sitting, was the reception, waiting room and doctor's cabin all rolled into one.

In this general area, I sat on a long wooden bench, waiting. My eyes rested on the framed medical posters on the opposite wall. A huge illustration of an infected penis highlighted the effects of STDs in men; another one showed a giant, infected vagina. Seeing the grotesque genitals made me feel disgusted about my work. Unable to bear the sight any longer, I looked away.

Thirty minutes passed. Where was Kanchan Bala? I began suspecting that something fishy was going on inside. I could not comprehend how a routine examination could take so long. Even from behind the partition, there was no sound. The stillness of the streets at that late hour made the silence even more alarming. I ran out of patience.

I knocked on the wooden partition. A few moments passed before it rolled open. The doctor emerged with a smile on his face. He pointed to an empty chair and sat behind a rickety table. I pulled the chair and sat on the edge. Where was Kanchan Bala!

'Relax,' he said with a beatific smile, seeing the desperation on my face. 'I have sent your friend back to Pathankot.'

I gawked at him like a goldfish.

'I have given her a shot. That should relieve at least 50 per cent of the pain. She will need two more, but there's nothing to worry about, sister. I have given her a prescription. She can take the shots back in her village.'

Slowly, I managed to focus on the story. So Kanchan Bala had flown from her golden cage! But all she had in her purse was loose change. Without money—

'I've sent my compounder with her,' the doctor said, interrupting my thoughts. 'He will buy her a train ticket and give her Rs 100 for the journey home.'

I fell silent.

'Now I have one request,' he said, lowering his voice. I am not merely a doctor, I am also a social activist. Your friend sought my help. I did what I could. Please make sure that this does not come to light at least till the morning.'

I could not find anything to say: it had happened so fast! Right under my nose, Kanchan Bala had disappeared as smoothly as a coin disappears from a magician's palm. The doctor had whisked her out of the back door while I waited like a patsy.

But I was not upset. In fact, I was delighted. Kanchan Bala had not entered our profession of her free will. She had the right to escape—and when the opportunity presented itself, she took flight with the help of this social activist-doctor. As I walked back, I marvelled at what a crazy world Kamathipura was—where doctors did the work of the police, the police did the work of gangsters and gangsters ruled in place of our elected ministers. Everything was upside down. As I neared the brothel, I sent up a silent prayer to Yellamma for Kanchan Bala's success: if she failed, a violent death awaited her.

When I reached the brothel, Kallu Mamad glared dubiously at me. He clenched his jaws and flexed his arms menacingly as he got up from his stool. I could tell that he sensed something amiss, but his pin-sized brain could not figure out what. I coolly squirted red paan juice from my mouth on to the wall and walked past him. His suspicion was not unwarranted: he had noticed that I had company when leaving the brothel an hour before, but I had returned alone. It was not surprising that he should smell a rat. Before he could gather his sluggish thoughts into a cohesive question, I went skipping up the stairs.

In the hall, a global conference seemed to be in progress. People from many nations were in the crowd that night—jabbering, joking and quarrelling. A harsh-voiced girl chortled a piggish snort in one corner. I could spot at least three Arabs. There were five or six white faces. Judging by their uniforms, I'd say they were sailors on shore leave come to anchor their cocks. Most likely German or French, but I could not be certain because I did not understand their language. They were communicating with Bhagwan Das, the high-level pimp, in pidgin English-Hindi—and the universal sign language for all things sexual.

Bhagwan Das looked like an unremarkable middle-class Gujarati from Ahmedabad. He wore a long, white kurta that came down to his knees, partially covering his dhoti. He had a black turban on his head, crackling new Kolhapuri chappals on his feet and decades of experience behind him. From the lowly bylanes of Kamathipura to high-end Colaba, he supplied girls for every price and perversion. His 'photo album' also included a few actresses who were mostly reserved for politicians, builders and other glamour-struck clients who wanted to fuck a name rather than a person.

This was the same pimp I had once asked to find me a place in an air-conditioned bungalow. I noticed astonishment in his eyes when he saw me entering. Perhaps he had not expected that I would make it on my own to such a sophisticated place. But there I was.

I wanted a word with him. He was, after all, a useful man to know. If he wanted, he could pick up a ten-rupee cage girl and make her a posh call girl worth a thousand a night. It was said that he had an impeccable eye for

potting diamonds in the rough. I wonder why he had
ailed in my case?

But before I could approach him, my eyes fell upon an
miable face in the crowd—Sadoba! I smiled with recognition
nd the remembrances it brought back: both times the
ensitive boy had come with his gun fully loaded but had
misfired. Now, his face showed that he had resolved not to
eave the battlefield without victory. I, too, wanted to satisfy
his long-held fantasy.

Without wasting time, I led him straight into a cabin.
Hawk-eyed Salma Bi stood guard in the corridor, tracking
he movements of the girls and their clients. She barged into
our cabin. Sadoba took out his wallet from his jeans and
ooked at me questioningly.

'Only fifty,' I said.

He put five ten-rupee notes into Salma Bi's outstretched
hand and I closed the door behind her. Sadoba was sitting
on the edge of the bed. I noticed the creases on his forehead
deepening. His eyes wandered absently across the white walls
and stopped at a framed *Playboy* centrefold. The white pin-
up girl stood on one foot like a stork, her blonde hair falling
by her side.

I sat down beside Sadoba.

'You like beer?'

He nodded.

'Would you like one now?'

He didn't say no.

I got off the bed and went out to get a bottle from Salma
Bi's stock. Besides sodas and colas, we also kept a supply of
beer, whisky, rum, charas and ganja. To access them, clients

were supposed to cough up double the market rate, but fo
Sadoba I paid from my own pocket.

I poured some beer into a mug and handed it to him.

'You won't drink?' Sadoba asked, as he took his firs
tentative sip.

'My job is to serve my master,' I replied, looking him i
the eyes.

He averted his eyes, grinning like a blushing schoolboy.

After a few sips, the wrinkles on his forehead ease
up. Before the first mug was drained, I was happy to se
his confidence begin to swell, along with the bulge in hi
crotch.

He soon began to jabber. He was the son of a leftis
trade union leader, he said, the right-hand man of Georg
Fernandes. Very powerful. Did I know George Fernandes
Without waiting for a reply, he continued. He was in hi
second year at college. Girls in college were all boring—two
plaited, oiled-hair girls with middle partings. He had thre
more years to go. After completing his degree, he planned to
join a chartered accountant's firm. Then he would make a lo
of money and come to me every week.

While he prattled on without a pause, I gently playe
with the different parts of his body, especially between hi
legs. I could feel him growing full and hard inside his pants
Before his second glass was through, he leaped on me like
hound in heat.

At that very moment, someone banged on the cabin doo
violently. All my efforts went to waste. Sadoba's intoxicate
passion was jerked back to sober reality. His penis shrunk lik
a pricked balloon.

The pounding on the door did not stop. Enraged, I hastily threw on my clothes and opened the door. Salma Bi was standing there with three of Babu Rao's thugs, including blotchy-faced Kallu Mamad. One of the men grabbed my wrist and dragged me to an unoccupied cabin. Slamming the door shut, Salma Bi asked point-blank, 'Where is Kanchan Bala!'

So they had figured out that their precious bird had flown away from the golden cage. Babu Rao had hand-picked each girl for this brothel and paid without negotiation. If one girl escaped, it set him back by at least Rs 3000.

'Isn't she here?' I asked innocently.

'No,' Salma Bi replied coldly.

'Then how would I know where she is?'

'She went out with you.'

Salma Bi's eyes were desperately searching my face for any clue of complicity. I could feel the eyes of the three goons scanning my face for the smallest flitter of fear.

I continued bluffing confidently, dishing out a partially true, partially concocted version of the night's events. 'It's true,' I said, 'that she went out with me. I had taken her to a doctor because she wasn't feeling well. The doctor wrote out a prescription for her, which she took to the chemist while I went to the paan shop and came back straight here. Did she really not return?'

I could see that my story had put all of them in a bind. Salma Bi turned to look at the goons. They looked at each other. No one answered my question.

Sensing my chance, I left them in their distressed state and returned to the cabin where I had left Sadoba. I had little reason to hope that he would be waiting for me on the bed after what had happened. When I pushed the door open, I found the boy gone. Third time unlucky. I shut the door sadly.

The following day, I learned that Babu Rao's goondas had searched high heaven for Kanchan Bala. The search party had first combed all her regular haunts. After that, they had rushed to the central railway stations. One thug had left for Victoria Terminus, another had gone to Dadar and the third to Bombay Central. For hours, they had paced up and down the railway platforms but had been unable to spot her. Kanchan Bala had successfully escaped.

This was not a bad way to extract revenge on Babu Rao. I considered it deeply. If I helped a few more girls escape, Babu Rao's damages would stand to be at least fifteen to twenty thousand rupees. Not to mention the incalculable harm to his reputation.

Razing Babu Rao's empire to the ground would be the first spark I would cause.

11

There were fifteen girls in our air-conditioned brothel. After Kanchan Bala's escape, fourteen remained. I had to find out what was brewing inside each of them. It was also imperative to win their trust. I was confident that I was up to the challenge.

I gradually began spreading my net. Up until then, I had kept a distance from the other girls. Partly because I considered myself a cut above them, and partly because they bored me. I did not participate in their juvenile jabbering about film stars or their bawdy banter about customers. I did not join them when they were glued together in bitchy little circles, stewing gossip from all corners of Kamathipura. Even when they went for a movie, I had refused to accompany them so many times they stopped asking. They had concluded that I was a snob, as well as an A-grade bitch. I hadn't cared less until then, but now I would have to change their opinion about me.

I began working earnestly towards it, offering a hand when they were oiling their hair, tweezing their eyebrows or bleaching their faces. In a matter of just a few weeks,

I became part of every leisure plan, every lewd joke and every loud gossip session. By and by, they started believing that I was part of their gang. Sure, Babu Rao still worshipped the ground I walked on, but apart from that I was one of them.

Since Kanchan Bala had fled, Babu Rao hadn't come over. Then one Sunday evening, he dropped in without warning. As soon as he entered, I threw myself at his service. He had a private room in the house where no one else was allowed. Entering the room, he pulled off his shirt and tossed it on the chair. As always, he wore a white *sando* banian under it. He did not consider it necessary to take off his shoes. With his heavy boots, he sprawled across the white bed.

I picked up his shirt and hung it neatly on a hanger. After putting it away in the wardrobe, I made him a peg of whisky, put the glass on a trolley together with the bottle and a thermos containing ice, and wheeled the trolley up to him. I placed myself at his feet like a devoted wife awaiting his command. I noticed that he had come back exhausted that night and seemed to be lost in his own world.

'What's on your mind, Rao?' I murmured, untying the laces of his right shoe.

He stretched out his arm to pick up the whisky glass from the trolley and sat up against the wall. 'That *gaandu*, Lala . . . He is a pain in the backside.' He sighed. 'Until I trap the bastard and finish him, I can't move ahead. Just one opportunity, that's all I need.'

His confiding in me was reassurance that he didn't suspect my involvement in the Kanchan Bala episode. 'Is there anything I can do to help?' I asked, as I eased off both his shoes and slipped them under the bed.

'Had your Sattar been alive, maybe we could have used him.'

A shudder travelled down my back upon hearing Sattar's name. With some effort, I controlled myself. 'Oh! When did he die?'

'Actually, even if he was alive, he would be of no use to anyone,' Babu Rao continued gruffly, as he gulped down the rest of his whisky. 'My boys beat him up good. They broke both his arms at the elbows . . .'

I bit my lip and persisted, asking cautiously, 'But where is he?'

'That's a mystery even to me.'

He sat up to make himself another drink. 'Had Sattar been here and still been besotted with you, we could have used him as a *khabri* to find out Lala's secrets.'

'What exactly do you want to know?'

Babu Rao swirled a mouthful of whisky as his eyes locked on to mine. The whisky seemed to be doing its job as a lubricant. Words started slipping out of his mouth. 'See, all these countries in the Middle East are crazy about goat's meat from India . . .'

The essence of what he said was that Rehmat Khan Lala exported goat's meat to almost every Middle Eastern country. The goats were slaughtered strictly in accordance with halal customs, skinned and flown to these countries on chartered planes. His agents there supplied the mutton to hotels and local markets. This was public knowledge. What Babu Rao was desperate to find out was whether packets of narcotics were sewn into the bodies of the headless goats. And whether, in return, Lala received payment in gold biscuits.

Babu Rao suspected—based on an unreliable informant's claim—but wanted to be dead sure before he acted on it. His plan was to nail Lala for life by passing this information on to the Narcotics Bureau.

I heard Babu Rao out with rapt attention. Then I suggested a plan. 'Rao, if you can find out where Sattar is, I can extract all this information from him. He must know all this. After all, he was Dawood's right hand. When we last met, he had confided that he was learning how to drive a car. Once he got his licence, he said he would be transporting mutton from the Deonar abattoir to the airport.'

'Hmm . . .' After giving it serious thought, Babu Rao replied, 'Give me some time . . . I will see what I can do.' His words, though, sounded hollow. I sensed that even he doubted if he could locate Sattar. Also, he didn't seem convinced that Sattar, even if found, would prove to be useful.

Within a few days, I had ferreted out the secrets of three of the brothel girls—Ruby, Mira and Radha. They were constantly giggling. A few times I noticed them laughing uproariously even at pedestrian jokes. Their cheerfulness was clearly a facade.

Mingling with them, I soon realized they were extremely unhappy. To mask their anguish, they stretched a smile across their powdered faces. I decided to dig deeper into their hearts.

I first invited Ruby, the most innocent looking of the trio, out for lunch. Skinny as a rumali roti, she was petite and had an angular face with full lips. She wore neon dupattas

every day, but her big baleful eyes belied that facade of sunny
cheer. Today, she was dressed in an azure floral maxi with
three coin-sized black buttons in the front.

'I don't step out without a rose in my hair,' she said, as we
walked down to an Irani restaurant. 'And a red bindi. With
a rose and a bindi, I feel like a complete woman . . . like I'm
walking on sunbeams.'

But what she disclosed to me half an hour later, in strict
confidence, was exactly the opposite. She was depressed and
suicidal. At their old brothel, the trio had once tried to flee
but their attempt had failed. They had been lashed until their
naked backs dripped blood like summer sweat. The brothel
owner had been glad when Babu Rao picked them.

Seeing her innocent face crumpling like a ball of paper,
I put an arm around her. While she ate, I told her tales of
Rani Laxmibai and Jijamata, which Aai had told me. I assured
her that victory would be hers in the end. I also promised to
stand by her like an elder sister if she needed support. My
words seemed to fill her deflated body and soul with renewed
hope. As I continued showing her visions of life outside the
wretched semen gutter, I could see glorious manifestations of
escape rising in her eyes again.

A few days later, once I had made sufficient inroads
with the other two girls too, I invited them to the Chinese
restaurant downstairs. Kajal-eyed Radha was attractive,
though she always dressed carelessly in a dark crumpled sari.
Her hair, which reached below her waist, was invariably
tangled up in knots. Curvy Mira, on the other hand, was
scrupulously neat and extremely particular when it came to
her appearance. Her hips were broad enough, as villagers

would say, to bear a thousand and one sons. She was proud of her ample figure despite both her breasts being inflicted with burns for daring to plan an escape.

I treated them to a lavish lunch with unlimited beer. Within half an hour of giggling, the walls began crumbling. Another beer and the trio revealed new plans of escaping. They said they wished to be home for Diwali but had not hit upon a fool-proof escape plan yet. I suggested that, this time, instead of trying to do everything themselves, they should take the help of a trustworthy and experienced outsider . . . perhaps a social activist. They liked the idea and asked me if I knew any such person—they would be ready to pay handsomely. I gave them the address of Dr Pritamlal and told him he would do it for free. Their eyes widened in eternal thanks.

Diwali week was boom-time in Kamathipura. Wallets warmed with crisp banknotes, men walked into our district with a swagger. A festive spirit lit the air. These were the days when we were tipped handsomely and regular clients bought trinkets and gifts for their girls.

A day before Diwali, I was surprised to see Devi entering our brothel.

'Hey!' I teased her. 'Have you lost your way?'

She grinned and handed me a shiny ribbon-tied box. 'This is from Maa . . . a Diwali gift for you.'

It was a pleasant surprise: I didn't work for Gangu Bai any more and had not kept up ties with her either. Despite that, she had remembered to send me a beautiful sari.

Every Diwali, Gangu Bai ordered around 200 saris. Of these, 150 were for the girls at her brothel. The rest were hand-delivered to those who had left for more posh establishments or had retired. Gangu Bai rarely forgot anyone.

Thinking about her, I began missing my Aai. She had written to me just twice since returning to Tulu. Both letters had been brief. The first one informed me that she had reached home safely. Kumkum was also doing well. The second envelope from her carried the receipt of the money I had wired.

I had earned Rs 6000 as a result of the deal between Babu Rao and Gangu Bai. Out of that princely sum, I had kept only Rs 1000 and returned the balance to Gangu Bai, requesting her to dispatch it to my mother. Aai had written to confirm that the money order had reached her.

I wrote her a detailed letter in reply. My life had certainly leapt forward since she had left Bombay. At Babu Rao's air-conditioned bungalow, my rates had tripled. I also wrote confidently that this was not yet the final stop in my journey. Like Aaji, and the proud women before her, I was born for marbled palaces—not for cages and warehouses. I was soon going to become a sophisticated call girl, fixing appointments over the phone.

If I really became a call girl, I would have my own apartment with my own telephone and all the comforts of modern life, not a kholi in a decrepit chawl with open gutters. I would be living in a tip-top luxury neighbourhood where the balconies would be lined with flower pots. I would live alongside the millionaires of Peddar Road, Altamount Road, Warden Road, Nepean Sea Road . . .

As I walked down to the letterbox with the envelope in my hand, I felt so charged that I could have lit up the whole of Bombay. I was certain that when Aai would read my letter, she would cry big, fat tears of joy.

After posting it, instead of going back, I walked to Gangu Bai's brothel. It was 7 p.m. and the streets of Kamathipura were coming to life. For Diwali, the fourteen lanes of the red-light district were lit up like ruby necklaces. Happy girls dressed in red and silver zari, as if they were the Diwali firecrackers themselves, wandered around like bright sparks.

This year, the Hindu festival of lights was overlapping with the Muslims' Eid celebrations, which was to follow just five days later. The girls hotly anticipated raking in double the money. The crowd had been swelling since the last fifteen days. The girls were well-prepared to deal with this rising tide. Like well-oiled machines, they worked round the clock: nights were packed and even during the day, clients would drop by for some holiday cheer.

Recently, an interesting topic had become the subject of discussion in our air-conditioned bungalow. One of the girls had asked: 'How were daytime clients different from those who came at night?' As the girls had weighed in on the matter with their personal experiences, several insights had emerged.

The girls seemed to agree that those who came at night were real mards, while those who came during the day were, for various reasons, emasculated sissies. Majority of these losers were married and lived in terror of their wives—scared chutiyas who sneaked back home before the sunset curfew imposed by their brain-chewing wives.

The second type of men who visited brothels during the day consisted of men who came only to experience the infamous delights of Kamathipura from far-flung towns. Like the married men, they had to leave early too, though for more practical reasons. The third type consisted of nervous college boys who preferred to finish off their rendezvous in Kamathipura as fast as possible and rush back home. Not all college students, however, were scared of risking their reputation: some not only stayed back after sunset, but even slept in till dawn.

Reaching Gangu Bai's brothel, I stopped in my tracks when I saw the grand decorations. Ornate rangoli designs had been drawn on either side of the entrance, with diyas and petals around each. I peeped inside. It looked like a millionaire's daughter was getting married! Hundreds of round paper lampshades hung gaily from the high ceiling. The walls were decorated with fresh marigold torans and balloons, glittering stars and crepe paper festoons. Chains of lights were strung across the tops of the cabins. The doors to all the cabins were shut. Every available bench, chair and upturned crate was taken up by clients busy fondling girls while waiting for their turn. The entire place smelled of Diwali sweets and incense and girls' attar.

I climbed the stairs up to the first floor and was soon standing in front of Gangu Bai's door. I was surprised. When the entire warehouse was alive with jubilation, why was it dead silent here?

I pushed the partly open door and found Gangu Bai slumped in a chair, all alone. There was a bottle of whisky and a glass on the table. She was playing cards all by herself as she sipped on her drink. Her face brightened upon seeing me. 'Come, beti, come in.'

Quietly, I walked up to her and, not knowing what to do next, touched her feet.

'Happy, aren't you?' she inquired, after blessing me.

I nodded. 'I am grateful to you, Guru Maa.'

'Did you like the sari?'

I nodded again, my head still bowed.

'To tell you the truth,' she said, continuing with her unfinished card game, 'you are one lucky girl.'

I raised my eyes and looked questioningly at her.

'Babu Rao has fallen in love with you. He told me that after Diwali he is going to kick his mistress out of the Peddar Road apartment and shift you there.'

I was speechless.

'You are not happy to hear this?'

I answered in a soft voice, 'I am.'

'You won't forget old Gangu Bai once you have moved into that apartment, will you?'

'No.' I shook my head.

A tear shook loose and fell down. I hadn't realized that my eyes had teared up seeing how lonely this aristocratic lady was. Those she supported, fed and loved had deserted her tonight to be with their own family and friends. Babu Rao was celebrating Diwali with his family, while Rehmat Khan Lala was busy with Eid preparations. Others were busy celebrating elsewhere while she sat by herself in her dreary gambling den with a pack of cards and a glass of whisky for company. I realized that all she really had was her maternal love for us girls. And that night, all her daughters were busy minting money.

The air-conditioned bungalow was sultry and suffocating. The powdered faces of the girls did not reflect any of the joy of the ongoing festivities. Instead, there was a shushed sense of doom. They were clearly not comfortable chit-chatting with their clients; I could tell they were putting up an act. In one corner, a knot of girls was deliberating in muted, anxious tones. The entire scene appeared deathly serious—as if hidden inside one of the cabins was a fresh corpse.

I took a few more steps towards my room and bumped into Salma Bi in the corridor. I asked her the reason for the deathly pall. She began cursing the pandits who had chosen a bloody jinxed day to open our brothel doors for business. 'Every other day,' she cried, 'some calamity strikes us! Last month, it was that *chudail* Kanchan Bala. Now three more *randis* have disappeared without a trace.'

I felt a lightness travelling through my body: my plan was working! But I could not float away yet. Until I had destroyed Babu Rao completely, Sattar's killing would weigh me down every second with the weight of steel columns.

I walked to my room to change into a fresh set of clothes. Wearing a white scarf, white top and tight white bell-bottoms, I arrived in the hall again. The television had been turned off. I switched it on and sat on the sofa facing it.

A spirited dance performance was coming on Doordarshan. It struck me that whenever I sat down to watch television, I would catch a classical dance performance. In brothels, dance had become profane, but it was always meant to be sacred. That night, Sitara Devi was striking Kathak steps like lightning. My Aaji, too, had been a breathtaking Kathak dancer. I had never seen her, but I had heard stories from Aai of her red bindi and wild flowing hair. Aai said that sometimes when she danced, her presence would be as intimidating as a lioness, and at other times she could be as graceful as lovestruck Radha dancing for her Krishna. Seeing Sitara Devi, I was reminded of her.

I remembered my father too. I hadn't known his face either. Aai had told me that he had died before I was born. His death had been mysterious. His body, hacked into four pieces, had been recovered from a sugarcane field. The needle of suspicion had pointed to Constable Naik. Not only was he my father's friend but also my mother's lover. But owing to lack of evidence, the case had remained unsolved.

As I sat watching television, a client came and sat near me. I shifted my focus from the screen and threw a warm smile his way. He returned the smile, his thin moustache stretching. He looked under forty, but his hair had started thinning out from the front. His gentle eyes peered curiously from behind silver-rimmed round glasses, similar to those that Gandhi had worn. But unlike Gandhi, this gentleman wore faded jeans under a clean, freshly pressed kurta.

I said, 'There are so many girls here, but you chose me. That is very gracious of you. I am grateful.' My opening line had been a formality, but I could see that it had hit the mark.

His expression changed immediately. He was pleased, and not without reason.

Most girls of Kamathipura did not welcome clients with respect. A few months in those dark streets were enough to make a girl throw away basic pleasantries and become a hardened whore. Her aim then was not even to please her client in bed, but solely to rip him off. She simply became a cold, dead fish in bed, lifeless and disinterested while the man pumped her furiously. Not surprising that instead of pleasure, her client only found minor relief—only slightly better than morning bowel movement. Who would teach these girls that if the client went away feeling gratified, he would empty his pockets for her willingly and even come back for more?

Not all girls were such mercenary creatures though. Some did try to shower the client with charm, like the yesteryear courtesans. A good example was Ruby, one of the three girls who had fled. Like me, she tried to put her heart and soul into pleasing men. Unfortunately, her affectations carried the stench of a life lived in the gutter of Kamathipura. She would sidle up to a client and open with, 'Hai! Just standing next to you is setting my cunt on fire. Can't imagine what a stud bull like you would do to me in bed.' A discerning customer—or a decent customer—would turn up his nose at the stink of the sewer in her words.

Most other men were tickled by girls talking dirty. Her words were coarse but the feelings behind them were sincere, and her clients appreciated that.

This new client who was sitting beside me seemed like a decent man. He spoke little, and when he did speak, his manner was placid. 'A friend of mine had spotted you,' he confessed in response to my initial remark. 'I am simply following his footsteps.'

'Oh! And what is the name of this admirer of mine?'

'K.L. Shankar.'

I tried to recollect. It did sound familiar. I had certainly heard it before. When? Where? How many months ago? I could not remember.

Seeing the confusion on my face, the client tried to help me out. 'On the mahurat day, he was among the specially invited guests.'

It immediately came back to me. K.L. Shankar was the gentleman who had given me the nickname 'Cuckoo'. We had not had sex. I was pleased to find out that my conversation had impressed someone so much. As much as I was flattered, I was curious too. 'What did your friend tell you about me?' I asked, cautiously.

'I am a story writer. Shankar told me that you could be a fascinating character for my new script.'

'What's your name?'

'Aabid.'

'Do you write for films?'

'Yes.'

On the television, Sitara Devi's graceful Kathak programme had ended with a shower of applause, and was followed by a Kathakali performance. Two well-built dancers in dramatic green masks and elaborate headgear were warming up. An operatic dance-drama based on the Ramayana began to unfold. Red-bearded and bloody-eyed Ravana was circling Sita menacingly. Then, unexpectedly, he leapt at her and—

DHADAAM! The main door slammed open and Kallu Mamad burst into the hall dragging Ruby behind him. He strode purposefully across the floor with her and disappeared through the back door. My chest caved into itself. My mind reeled. Kallu's heavy steps had stamped out the bright smile from my face. I looked around and saw that the faces of the girls sitting with their clients had turned ashen too.

'Who was that girl?' Aabid couldn't contain his curiosity.

I composed myself and looked at him. 'She is another character for your story. If you stay here for a few days, I am sure you will find a thrilling story to write on brothel life.'

'Who will let me stay here?'

'Me!'

He stared at me with disbelief. I noticed that he looked only at my face, not once did his eyes wander down to my partially exposed bra.

'Ah! You are worried you won't be fully satisfied with my services?' I asked politely. Before he could reply, I continued, 'Well, you would be at ease if you allowed me to serve you for a few minutes.'

I intertwined my fingers with his as I got up. We entered the corridor and went straight into a cabin. I sat on the bed. He did not sit next to me. Instead, he chose to sit on a three-legged stool facing me. He was a strange one.

Looking at me through his round glasses, he smiled and explained politely, 'I have not come to satisfy the hunger that other men visit you for.'

I blinked. This was the first time I had come across a normal, healthy man who was willing to pay my full price but had no desire to touch me.

'Are you scared?'

'Scared of what?'

'Diseases . . . like syphilis. I'm completely clean. And anyway, I insist all my clients use a condom. So, you have absolutely no reason to be scared.'

Smiling, he began asking me questions about my life. Questions no one had asked me before. Some which even I had never asked myself. But whatever I said, he noted it down faithfully in his pocket diary. Thirty minutes later, he snapped the diary shut and counted out five notes of ten rupees on the bed. Before I could open my mouth, he said that if I didn't mind he would like to visit me again. And then he walked out.

I stared blankly at the money on the bed. Men were of so many different kinds. I thought of my father, Constable Naik, Bhajan Lal, Babu Rao, Rehmat Khan Lala, Sattar, and now this crazy character. Every man has a wild beast within him: some learn how to tame it and some are consumed by it.

12

Around 3 a.m., after servicing all their clients, the girls headed for their rooms. They were exhausted and it showed on their faces. They looked as if they would collapse. As long as the clients were around, they managed to pull through on the basis of sheer willpower. When the last client left, they realized that they barely had the energy to get up and move a single step.

I had just entered my room and hit the bed when the doors of all the cabins began to rattle violently—DHANDHANDHAN—one after the other. Terrified that some natural calamity had struck, the girls came running out, wondering what was going on!

Salma Bi was standing in the corridor, hands on her hips and a nasty look on her face. All the girls were given stern orders to move to the hall. This was unprecedented: never before had we been forcibly pulled out of our rooms after a hard night's work and ordered to assemble in the hall.

Cursing Salma Bi aloud, calling her a wrinkled old chudail and other choice abuses, the girls reluctantly trundled out.

They slumped into the sofas with sour faces. Dog-tired, I also collapsed into a single sofa seat. That was the beginning of the worst week of my life.

When all the girls had gathered in the hall, Kallu Mamad entered with Ruby. Everyone jumped. I was no exception. Ruby was stark naked. No rose in her hair, no red bindi on the forehead. *Without these two, a woman is incomplete*, her words echoed in my ears. I felt a shiver running through me as I looked at her. We were all used to seeing naked bodies, but Ruby's stripped and humiliated nakedness was different: it was like seeing a living corpse. The atmosphere was tense, the room was deathly silent and the air smelt of fear.

I still could not comprehend how Ruby had been caught. Also, how had Babu Rao's men managed to catch her alone? She had escaped with Mira and Radha. How had they fled while she was trapped?

Salma Bi was no less ruthless than Babu Rao's bulldogs. With a sadistic grin, she twisted Ruby's arm so hard that she was thrown off balance, on to the floor. Ruby attempted to get up, but Salma Bi kicked her hard in the ribs and in the face. She collapsed on to the carpeted floor, wheezing.

As Ruby lay on her stomach, it struck me that her body was too bruised for business, not for a few months at least. It became clear that they did not want her back in the brothel: they were planning to make an example of her—a cautionary tale. Sometimes, when a runaway was caught in Kamathipura, she was thrashed beyond repair, that too in front of her friends: others had to be made aware of the consequences.

Kallu Mamad had a bullwhip in his hand. He brought the spiked end cracking down on Ruby's bare back. She screamed. He rolled it up again. Ruby stood up and tried to cover herself. Kallu started raining lashes on her exposed body. Red-rimmed welts began to appear on her skin. Kallu continued mercilessly until she was on the floor, writhing in agony like a sacrificial goat whose neck has just been severed.

I was feeling frustrated at my own helplessness. Ruby was screaming before my very eyes and I could do nothing to save her. Salma Bi already suspected that I had helped Kanchan Bala escape. If she uncovered this secret as well, I would be the one on the carpet, naked and bleeding.

I considered my situation. To protect Ruby, I was prepared to surrender and face the repercussions. I was not afraid of the whipping, but that would neither help Ruby go scot-free nor would it help me get justice for Sattar. I had to make that happen. With every lash that landed on Ruby's broken body, I steeled my vow of vengeance against Babu Rao.

Through a curtain of furious tears, I watched as Ruby's back was bathed in blood—my heart too was bleeding. The whip had lacerated her back and caused her skin to fall apart like tissue paper. She had stopped writhing and moaning, and now lay motionless. Perhaps she had lost consciousness.

Kallu Mamad threw the bloodied whip aside and grabbed her by the hair. He dragged her as if she was a stray dog he had run over and dumped her on the floor of her room. Locking the door from outside, he returned to the hall. Picking up the whip, he proceeded to casually clean the blood from it with a chequered handkerchief and went to his post downstairs as if nothing had happened. All of us sat stunned.

After that night of agony, Ruby lay in her room without food or water for three days and three nights, groaning, and when the pain got unbearable, howling. Hearing her piteous sounds in the corridors, I felt like I would break down any moment. But I gritted my teeth and tried to keep a cool head. A hundred times every day, I repeated to myself that turning myself in would help neither Ruby, nor Sattar, nor me. I needed to hold on to my sanity for all our sakes.

Salma Bi neither called in a doctor for Ruby nor allowed us to apply haldi paste to her wounds. We were not even allowed to visit her. In our own rooms, in our own ways, we all prayed silently for our fallen sister.

On the fourth day, Ruby died. Babu Rao's men obtained a fake death certificate saying she had died of natural causes and dropped Ruby's corpse outside a government crematorium. Within minutes, Ruby was turned into ash.

A heavy blanket of silence descended upon all of us as we retreated into ourselves. It was not just Ruby who had suffered those three days. We, too, had felt the pain. We, too, had died a little with every moan of hers. Had Ruby lived a few more days, her aching cries would have pushed me to take my own life.

After Ruby's death, I did not feel like living in that air-conditioned prison—it was as if something in me had left with Ruby. I stayed in my room most of the time. There were two reasons for my grief. Ruby's painful death was the main one. A part of my mind taunted me that I was to blame—had I not encouraged her, she would not have died a dog's death. The second reason for my anguish was Sattar. I had done all I could to find him, but my attempts had yielded no result.

With the passage of time, Sattar was becoming like a pleasant memory from another lifetime. The bittersweet pictures of our relationship had begun to fade away into the distant horizon of history. It was as if I was sitting in the rear seat of a moving car, looking back and watching the world behind me getting lost in a fog.

With every passing day, my isolation deepened. Sometimes I felt like running away, but where would I go? There was no point going back to my village. Gangu Bai would not welcome me back after giving her word to Babu Rao.

And even if Gangu Bai did roll out the red carpet for me, Babu Rao would simply not allow it. He had fallen in love with me. Here, he had given me full freedom. There was no compulsion to even entertain clients. Babu Rao was taking care of all my expenses unstintingly. Another question that troubled me was: If I didn't do this work, what would I do all day? Chatting with clients at least occupied my mind for a few moments.

Meanwhile, my reputation continued to grow by leaps and bounds. Clients would come from far and wide, seeking our brothel and asking for me by name. Satisfied clients not only returned but also became publicity agents, referring unhappily married friends and lonely colleagues to me.

It was reaching a point where every evening clients would queue up for me before sunset. This was unheard of in Kamathipura. One reason for this frenzy was also my golden rule of not accepting more than ten clients a night. Knowing this, excited clients came early to grab their spot for that night.

The previous week, a Bengali jeweller had paid me a visit. Another client of mine, a friend of the jeweller, had praised me to the moon before him. Unfortunately, he was late—I had already entertained my last client for the night. I was sitting in the hall, watching television, when the jeweller, dressed in a silk dhoti and kurta, came quietly and sat down beside me. He first asked me my name to ensure that I was the right girl and then reached for his kurta pocket and took out his wallet.

'Not tonight,' I said politely. 'Come tomorrow, please.'

He was surprised. I told him about my ten-customer rule, but he was unwilling to budge. He placed a hundred-rupee note on the side table, offering me double my usual rate. I didn't accept it. He then placed another hundred-rupee note over the first one. Other girls walking past began stopping to watch the drama unfold. A gaggle of them gathered some distance away, looking at us with wide eyes.

The heap of hundred-rupee notes kept piling up. The jeweller kept adding a new note every few seconds, waiting to see if my reaction had changed. After he had emptied his wallet, he reached into another pocket and took out an envelope that was stuffed with a thick wad of fresh hundred-rupee notes.

He looked at me, eyebrows arched in question. I only smiled politely in response. It was becoming a battle of wills now. He continued adding to the pile, glancing at me each time he placed another note. Finally, he ran out of money. After throwing the last note, he said, 'Here is Rs 7500. Think about it . . . seven thousand five hundred!'

I stared at the money. I must confess I was sorely tempted in that moment. At the same time, my pride kicked in: my price had shot up from Rs 50 to Rs 7500 in a single night!

Calming my emotions, I picked up all the money and put it into the jeweller's pocket. His eyes opened saucer-wide. The expressions on the faces of the girls gathered around were not much different.

When Babu Rao learnt of this incident, he immediately shifted me from the air-conditioned brothel to his air-conditioned apartment on Peddar Road. The long side of the apartment overlooked the Arabian Sea. All day, all night, one could hear the gentle wash of the waves swishing in the background.

I had become the mistress of the man I hated from the bottom of my heart. But I did not have to worry about my sundry expenses any more. I would be given a thousand rupees every month as allowance. I did not have to worry about food or clothing either. Babu Rao would provide everything I desired.

Besides that, he had kept a maid to take care of me. Her job was to keep the apartment clean and cook whatever it was that I fancied. I had every conceivable comfort that Bombay's call girls enjoyed.

Salma Bi had dropped me to the apartment in a taxi. After breakfast, I had hurried to the Chinese beauty parlour to get my eyebrows done and body waxed. By evening, I was all set to welcome Babu Rao for the first night. I wore bright lipstick, but my outfit was unexpected. Instead of a predictable salwar-kameez, or even a bridal red sari, I decided to surprise him with a replica of Revolver Rani's costume!

I wore a felt hat and paired it with a yellow scarf around my neck, like the ones worn by British-era thugs. To complete the look, I put on a long-sleeved green shirt with two breast pockets, a broad leather belt with a dummy revolver in the holster, knee-length cowboy boots and skin-tight jeans. I had finally fulfilled my desire to dress up like Revolver Rani!

Babu Rao rang the doorbell earlier than I had expected. I checked the cuckoo clock in the drawing room—it was only seven-fifteen. I hid behind the bedroom door.

The maid opened the main door and scurried back into the kitchen, shutting the door behind her. Babu Rao's excited eyes scanned the drawing room as he stood at the entrance, searching for me. He took a few hesitant steps into the house and stopped. The faintest flicker of fear floated across his face.

Not giving him too much time to think, I burst out from my hiding place in my Revolver Rani avatar. Pointing my dummy pistol straight at his face, I yelled, 'Hands up in the air, Rao! You are under arrest.'

Rao froze. Frankly, I enjoyed seeing terror in his eyes. He was about to really surrender when I gave the game away—seeing his petrified face, I could not suppress a giggle. I had not expected this macho gangster to be such a coward. Even after I had burst into peals of laughter, the fear continued to linger on his face. The jolt had numbed him—as if Yamraj had just rung the doorbell by mistake. He did not take his wary eyes off my face, as if the gun might be real after all.

He took a few steps towards the bedroom and then changed his mind and sank into the sofa. I sat on his lap and gathered him in my arms. I still had the pistol in my hand.

'Did I scare you, jaanu?' I whispered into his ear.

He did not answer.

'How did you like my new clothes?' I tried again.

'Don't ever play such a prank on me again.'

'Why?'

'Behenchod, my heart almost stopped,' he muttered.

I took off my felt hat and set it on his head. I then handed him the revolver before taking off the yellow scarf and shirt, and unzipping my high boots. I loosened my belt and peeled off my jeans. Now, I was only in my bra and panties. I snuggled into his arms, pressing my chocolate-brown breasts against him.

He placed the revolver on the table and slipped one arm around me. 'You like the apartment?' he asked, attempting to steer the conversation to happier shores.

I bit his earlobe. 'You will get your answer in the bedroom.'

He beamed.

'Are you comfortable here? Any problems?' Getting his stride back, he put the felt hat on my head.

'Only one . . .'

He ran his eyes searchingly over my face.

'This apartment has everything I could ever want. Except you. And without you, all these comforts are meaningless to me.'

Flattered, he replied, 'I will try my best to spend more nights here.'

'How many?'

'Say . . . twice a week.'

'That's all?'

'I used to give Ivy only one night a month.'

I did not press him further.

Slipping out of his arms, I entered the bedroom. From the minibar cabinet in the wall, I picked a bottle of Johnny Walker and prepared a large peg for Babu Rao.

Babu Rao came in and sprawled on the bed in the half-light, his back supported by pillows. The two big swells of his muscular chest threw his flat stomach, hard as a board, in deep shadow. He had the body of a heavyweight boxer in his prime. I handed him the drink and sat beside him.

'Kumud,' Babu Rao said, as he took the first sip. 'Those whom I love, I shower with money.' His words did carry the fragrance of affection, but they were followed by a threat. 'And those whom I hate, I make sure they rot in hell.'

'Rao, you have only showered me with your love so far.'

'No, no, no. You have known just a drop of it.'

'And in which birth will I have the good fortune of drowning in the ocean of all your love?'

'In this birth. Once my new business is successful.'

The 'new business' part was not clear to me, so he explained. He was entering the big league now! He had struck a deal with a sheikh in Dubai. A ship carrying gold biscuits worth Rs 45 lakh was to arrive in Bombay shortly.

Babu Rao had juiced all his political contacts. He had already bribed senior police officials and greased palms in the customs as well. He had already spent a fortune on this, paying out Rs 1 lakh to each official. He had planned every step with meticulous care and believed that his plan had a 99 per cent chance of succeeding. Of course, he said, it's always that 1 per cent which seals our fate. The vessel could be shipwrecked in a storm and all the gold could sink to the bottom of the Arabian Sea. Or some CBI officers in Delhi could wake up and decide to raid the ship. That would mean the end of Babu Rao. He had invested practically everything he had into this all-or-nothing gamble. Not only that, he had also taken loans from loan sharks and illegal bankers.

And if he succeeded? Overnight, he would have more money flowing through his hands than there was sewage in Kamathipura's drains. He would become far richer than Rehmat Khan Lala. With this money, he would line the pockets of Lala's key men and become the undisputed ruler of Kamathipura. If things went according to Babu Rao's plan, before long, Rehmat Khan Lala would be deported back to Kabul.

Babu Rao was in the process of fine-tuning his plan to make it watertight. He had all the necessary information. He had confirmed information by then that Rehmat Khan Lala's headless halal goats were merely packaging for the narcotics he smuggled into the Middle East.

After four pegs, Babu Rao picked up the whisky bottle and began swigging it down in large gulps. Now that he was drunk, he began blabbering. From his impassioned words, I realized that he was indeed in love with me. He wanted to take me around the world on a luxury liner. He declared that if the situation ever arose, he would not flinch from sacrificing his life for me.

And that was the truth. Drunkards don't lie. I unzipped his jeans and took them off. He wanted me to suck him first. Within minutes, he was moaning. Sufficiently hard, he got on top of me and spread my arms outwards. I held on as he began hammering hard into me. It was my turn to moan, pretending as if I was loving every minute of it.

I tried to distance my mind from my body and wondered how he would react if he came to know the truth about my feelings for him: not only did I not love him, but I curdled at his touch. He would get such a shock that he would strip me like Ruby and lash me with his own hands. This horrific image sent a shiver down my body, just as Babu Rao spurted his useless seed inside me.

The following day, I got a postcard from Aai. It had originally been sent to Gangu Bai's address. One of the girls there had redirected it. The postcard—criss-crossed with postal marks and rubber stamps—had been written more than a month earlier.

Aai had written that she had contracted a fatal disease which was eating into her lungs. One lung had become almost useless. The doctors had advised surgery, but Aai did not want to be cut up. She wanted me to come home for at least a few days—though I knew she hoped I would stay and hold her hand till her last day.

I was worried. Aai had nobody by her side, except Constable Naik's daughter. But at fourteen, she was still naïve. There was no one else in the neighbourhood upon whom Aai could rely.

My problem was that the coming month was critical. There was no way I could leave Bombay. Several matters required urgent action. The most important of these was to find a way to secretly meet Rehmat Khan Lala.

I had conceived a plan to extract the perfect revenge on Babu Rao. This was the time I had been waiting for. This was the situation I had been waiting for. One precise blow and Babu Rao would be roaming the streets of Kamathipura with a begging bowl. My heart would not let me rest until I had brought Babu Rao to utter ruin.

13

Babu Rao had employed a Christian maid for me. The day I stepped into the apartment, I knew that she had been instructed to keep a careful eye on me. I had no doubt that she reported my daily activities in detail. If I were to invite a man to the apartment in Babu Rao's absence, it would prove to be the biggest mistake of my life.

This is where Babu Rao's former mistress, Ivy, had erred. She had got involved with a younger man who visited her every Saturday morning. If the maid was shrewd, the mistress was no simpleton either. During the time of her rendezvous, she would send the maid out of the house on an errand that would keep her away for at least two to three hours.

A few Saturdays passed this way, without incident. But soon, the maid began to wonder why she was being kicked out of the house only on Saturday mornings.

One Saturday, an hour earlier than expected, she quietly opened the door with her key and tiptoed into the apartment. Ivy, caught with her young paramour, pants down, got the shock of her life. She jumped out of bed and tried to buy her silence with ten crisp hundred-rupee notes. The maid accepted the cash wordlessly but went ahead and did what she was expected to anyway. Ivy was unceremoniously kicked out of the house, and I was brought in.

My solitude in the apartment was as unrelenting as the roar of the ocean waves. I was cut off from all my clients. I could no longer offer pleasure or warmth to any man other than Babu Rao. I had all the comforts I could ask for, but time trickled by as slowly as tar.

Such was my new life.

To pass time, I took to watching a movie every day. I took the maid along whenever I stepped out. We would often dine together at fancy restaurants. I would also buy her small gifts every once in a while.

The gifts I bought to win the maid's confidence were a pittance compared to the gifts Babu Rao gave me as offerings of his devotion. Every time he visited me, he brought me a gold ornament or an expensive sari. The previous week, it was a pendant watch. The week before, it had been a bottle of Chanel No. 5 perfume, which he said famous Hollywood actresses wore to bed.

Like a devoted wife, I would often chide him for his extravagance. 'Rao, for heaven's sake, please stop it. I know that you are going through a lean phase. All your funds have been invested in the new venture. Once the plan meets with success, you can gift me the whole of Bombay, I won't object.'

Babu Rao's vanity would be tickled by my loving reprimands. Like a sahib at the racecourse, who owned a purebred Arabian horse, he would glow with pride. When Rao would walk away, I would observe his gait. It thrilled me to notice that his steps were that of a man intoxicated—or sometimes, of a man with no earth under his feet. Babu Rao was floating on the clouds. I couldn't wait to bring him down to earth.

Another week dragged by. I had not found any source that could help me contact Rehmat Khan Lala. I knew the addresses of the addas he owned around Kamathipura, but I could no longer visit those places, not even concealed under a hijab. If anyone spotted me in Lala's territory, my fate would be sealed.

A week later, holding a hastily scribbled address, Aabid found his way to my door. As I mentioned, he was a friend of producer K.L. Shankar and wrote stories and scripts for films. He had met me once at the air-conditioned bungalow, where he had asked me questions about my life for half an hour and left. Why would the maid or Rao object to such a harmless creature whose sole interest was my life story, not my body?

I made Aabid comfortable on the drawing-room sofa and went into the kitchen.

'Who's that?' the maid asked, as she took the pressure cooker off the stove.

'Aabid, a writer. He wants to write the story of my life for a film . . . from the pavement to Peddar Road.' She appeared unamused, so I tried to tempt her with a carrot. 'And since you are a part of my life, he will certainly add your character too.'

She shot a dubious glance at me before lifting the pressure regulator off the lid. Hot steam foamed around the body of the cooker before evaporating.

'Do you think,' I asked innocently, 'Rao Sahib would mind his presence here?'

She smiled tightly before shaking her head.

'Come on then, make us some coffee and join us in the hall.'

With this, I dispelled any last doubts lingering in her mind. I returned to the hall and sat on the sofa, facing Aabid.

'How are you?' I asked him.

'What a fancy place!' he said, craning his neck to take in the richly furnished drawing room. 'Your rates must have shot up sky-high . . .'

'Not at all.'

He stopped and looked at me, his eyebrows knotted together in puzzlement.

I smiled. 'There are no rates any more.'

His eyes were still fixed on my face, bewildered. As the maid walked in with coffee, I explained that I was not on the market any more—my body and life were devoted only to my Babu Rao Sahib. From the corner of my eye, I could sense the maid was gratified. To Aabid, I added, 'You are a friend. Drop in whenever you feel like it.'

Reassured by his brotherly manner and the safe distance we kept from each other, the maid placed the tray on the centre table and went back into the kitchen.

I picked a cup from the tray and offered it to Aabid, asking, 'How is your story progressing?'

'I've yet to put pen to paper.'

'When do you plan to begin?' I picked up the other cup.

'I will decide after our meeting today,' he answered, looking at me above the rim of his cup. 'No doubt, so far, you have led a fascinating life.'

Sipping his coffee, he continued, 'There is a vast difference between the Kumud who solicited customers in the dark alleys of Kamathipura for two rupees and the Kumud who lives in a luxury apartment—and tells me she is priceless!'

'Not really. Kumud is the same. Only the backdrop has changed.'

'That is also true,' he agreed, cleaning his Gandhi-like glasses with a handkerchief. 'But seeing where you have ended up, anyone would be jealous.'

'This is not my ending. This is just the starting point.'

He blinked as he put his glasses back on. 'My God! If this big, fancy house is the beginning, where do you think it will end?'

'On the silver screen.'

'What!'

'I want to be in films. I want to be a heroine . . . like Madhubala.'

Putting my empty cup on the tray, I cautiously said, 'If I am not mistaken, the scripts you have written haven't been made into films so far.'

He drew in a long breath and sighed, finishing his coffee in two swallows.

I had hit a vein of truth. 'You are struggling hard though . . .'

Studying his empty coffee cup, he uneasily admitted, 'You are right. For the past five years, I have been knocking on every door. But the padlock of kismet is yet to open even a crack!'

'It will. You won't have to wait long now.'

'Why do you say that?'

I leaned back on the sofa and stared at him levelly.

'This story you are writing about my life . . . it is my responsibility to see that it goes on the floors.'

I cannot say for sure whether he believed me, but for the next few days and nights, he threw himself into writing with the passion of a dervish. Two days later, he returned with a brief outline of the story. He narrated it to me. For me, there was nothing new in it. It didn't feel novel or exciting. Perhaps because it was the story of my own life.

In short, the story began with my childhood days back in Tulu. According to the story, as a child, I loved birds. But not birds in cages. So, I opened the bird-catcher's cages secretly at night and set them free. One summer, I was transported to Bombay in a truck and struggled to survive in the violent lanes of Kamathipura. There was a special mention of Champa, my childhood friend who became a crone at the age of twenty-three. Truck driver Bhajan Lal, who was brutally knifed by Dawood Khan, was also an important character.

Sattar's character was presented as my lover. However, Aabid couldn't figure out how to tie up the loose ends. This was expected. Sattar's fate was still a mystery. Aabid strongly believed that if he could find out what had really happened to Sattar, the story would have a satisfying climax. The rest of the story was so real, he didn't want to spoil the end with a filmy cliché.

'Okay then,' I said, after listening to all his points patiently. 'I will find a fitting climax for your story.'

'You know it?'

'If you cooperate, along with the climax, I will also find you a very wealthy financier for your film.'

He sat up straight. I could see gelatin-silver visions of his cinema future twinkling in his eyes. I had answered his prayers! Now I was certain that he would be ready to walk on fire if I asked.

I got down to business straight away. Lowering my voice a notch, I told him that his part of the deal was to fix a meeting between Rehmat Khan Lala and myself. 'Just the two of us,' I quietly underlined. He did not decline. I gave him the address of one of Lala's liquor dens. From there, he would have to find a way of reaching the underworld don.

He silently absorbed everything I was saying. I took his silence as an expression of consent and clarified a few more points. Once he met Lala, I told him, he was to whisper into his ears that Kumud wanted to see him in private. For a wise man, a hint is enough.

At last, Aabid opened his mouth. 'Is that all?'

'Yes, that's it.'

The wheels of Babu Rao's ruin had started turning. I voluntarily caged myself in the apartment and instructed Aabid to call as soon as he had something to report, instead of dropping in, so as not to give the maid the slightest cause for suspicion. I was afraid the phone would ring when we were out shopping, or at the cinema. So I spent the whole day on the sofa near the phone, reading my Marathi books or standing on the balcony watching the waves crashing. If I left the drawing room, I would position myself in such a way that the phone was within sight. Once every hour, I would lift up the receiver to confirm it was working—hearing the dial tone, I would put it down, satisfied. For the next few days, the telephone became the centre of my existence.

A whole day and a whole night passed by. The next day dawned and the minutes began crawling again. To pass time, I watched the sea birds, but the seconds seemed like minutes and the minutes hours. It seemed like eternity until the sun began dipping in a blazing saffron-streaked purple sky. I continued to wait until the trees had turned into dark silhouettes against the last flares of the setting sun. The call did not come.

Babu Rao did.

For a few moments, I stared blankly at him. His sudden appearance had caught me unawares. 'What's the problem?' he asked, perplexed.

'After how many days have you shown up?'

'Just five days, darling.'

'For you, they are just five days,' I said, putting my arms around his hips. 'For me, they are like five years.'

Before he could say anything, I silenced his mouth with a kiss so deep that I almost suffocated on stale Old Spice aftershave. We went into the drawing room. He sat on the sofa and I, as usual, nestled in his lap like a kitten.

'Tell me,' I asked, playfully stroking the knotty hair on his chest, 'what shall I serve you tonight . . . whisky, vodka, rum or gin?'

'Tonight is a night for rum!' he said gleefully. 'But after we return.'

'Oh! Are we going out to dinner?'

In reply, he produced a string of movie tickets from his pocket and waved them at my face. 'I'm taking my queen for the late show tonight! I've booked the last row for us.'

My breath stopped. I did not want to leave the apartment even for a moment, and he planned to take me out for at least three hours, if not more.

'No!' I declared petulantly, rising from his lap. 'I won't go.'

He was taken aback. 'Almost every day you go to watch a movie with the maid,' he protested. 'And with me . . .?'

'You are so busy with your work all day! You never spare a thought that your beloved might need a distraction from the pain of pining for you. If you lived here with me, I would never dream of going out, Rao. I would simply keep looking into your eyes.'

He ignored what I had said. Like an adamant child, he whined that at least this once I should accompany him. He had bought the tickets out of love and wanted to watch this movie only with me. I felt helpless. If I pricked his fragile male pride at this point, my future plans could go awry.

He waited on the drawing room sofa, legs stretched out on the centre table, while I went to the bedroom to change. Babu Rao's favourite colour was purple, so I wore a raw silk aubergine-coloured sari with a matching blouse. His golden pendant watch gleamed at my cleavage. I sprayed on some Chanel No. 5 and returned to the drawing room in a cloud of fragrance.

I had deliberately left the top two hooks of my blouse unfastened. I stood close to Babu Rao and turned my back suggestively. He stood up and moved his thick fingers to hold the clasp. As he hooked the buttons, I allowed myself a fantasy about fulfilling my promise to Sattar and smiled to myself.

I was rudely brought back to reality by the shrill ring of the telephone—I froze!

Babu Rao was standing right next to it. He reached out and picked up the receiver. My heart was racing. I knew whose call it was.

'Who's speaking?' Babu Rao asked gruffly. He remained silent for almost a minute. I could hear staccato crackling sounds from the other end; Aabid was explaining something. Finally, Babu Rao turned to me and said flatly, 'Someone for you.'

'Oh, is it? Must be Aabid, the writer,' the words spilled out of my mouth as I grabbed the receiver. 'Aabid Bhai,' I said, emphasizing the word 'bhai', 'I am just going out with my man. Right now, I have no time to discuss your story. Please call me in the morning. You will, won't you?' I hung up before Aabid could respond.

'Who is this writer?' Babu Rao asked as we proceeded towards the door. I had expected this question. I told him in brief about Aabid's plan to write a script for a film based on my life. I also mentioned how he had dropped into the flat once to clarify some details, how he had asked me a few questions, jotted down the answers and left.

'Why did he call now?' Rao asked, stepping into the lift.

'The story must have got stuck somewhere. He probably wanted to know some details about my old business!'

'Ummm,' he mumbled, as if he had yet to determine whether he was fully satisfied with my reply.

We reached the ground floor and got into the car to drive to Eros Theatre. I was expecting an English movie because that is what the cinema generally screened. However, this week, it was a Hindi movie. Ironically, the movie was called *Shaque*, suspicion.

How apt! I was doing all I could to ward off any suspicion. Meanwhile, in the movie, the worm of doubt had quietly started burrowing its way into the heroine's mind. She suspected her husband of infidelity.

It was a new experience to have the entire row to ourselves in a houseful theatre, but I could not focus on the movie. The reason was that as soon as the lights dimmed, Babu Rao put his left hand suggestively on my thigh. I was suddenly thrown back to the memory of Sattar hesitantly placing his hand on me during our first movie. I remembered the tremor I had felt, how he had made me feel. I remembered how he had made me feel like a girl who had just turned sixteen. And then Babu Rao's fingers reached inside my thighs and the shiver turned into one of distaste. Every day, I longed for when my vengeance would be complete and this accursed burden would be lifted from my shoulders.

After the movie, Babu Rao had planned another surprise for me. For dinner, he took me to Hotel Blue Nile. The jazz cabaret was in full swing when we entered the dimly lit hall. A topless dancer was prancing across the stage, swaying her hips and shoulders. Her movements were picked out by a coloured spotlight. A chiffon scarf swathed her hips as she moved her bare breasts to the beat. Her half-naked body was as smooth and unblemished as a porcelain doll. With her outstretched arms, she dared the men to come and ravish her. But, of course, no one there had the courage: they looked and applauded and ate their dinner. Had she been in Kamathipura, the truck drivers would have been riding her with the same recklessness with which they drove on highways.

We found ourselves an empty table. The dancer's glittering necklace caught my eye. It was beautiful. Babu Rao was gazing at me, trying to read my face. He had noticed I had been a little distracted during the movie. I took my eyes off the dancer and glanced at him.

'You like the necklace?' he asked.

I fluttered my eyelashes. Then, flashing a smile, I added, 'You seem very happy today!'

His eyes gleamed as he whispered excitedly, 'The ship from Dubai will reach the Bombay docks next week. I received a telegram this morning!'

A waiter approached us and handed us the menu. Babu Rao was illiterate. I, too, did not have much of an education. However, I did have the advantage of having studied in the village school till the fourth grade. I went through the menu and placed the order for both of us.

The cabaret dancer was now sashaying around in the maze of tables, weaving and gyrating. Matching the rhythm of the jazz beats, she was jiggling every part of her body, and swaying forward and backwards provocatively.

She then made her way to our table. When she leaned in close, Babu Rao simply reached out and tore the necklace off her neck. The poor girl was shocked!

Babu Rao then handed me the necklace and opened his wallet before the girl. '*Kitna?*' he asked. She was still dazed and kept staring at him blankly. The people around us began nudging each other and turning to stare. 'How much?' Babu Rao asked again, firmly this time. Coming to her senses, the girl murmured, 'Fifteen hundred.'

Babu Rao extracted two large amber-red thousand-rupee notes from his wallet and offered them to the girl. Her eyes widened even further with surprise.

Babu Rao was not just in love, but madly in love with me. If love was a ladder, he was teetering dangerously at the top. Had I asked for the moon, he would have brought it down for me with a handful of stars as well.

I, however, didn't feel anything even remotely resembling love for him. I lived with a venom even snakes would die from—but it was essential that I, too, express love just as clearly to him. I needed him to remain convinced that my passion not only matched his, but that I was two steps ahead of him in my single-minded devotion.

Before dinner, the waiter brought us a bottle of chilled beer with a glass. I requested him to bring one more glass. Now it was Babu Rao's turn to be surprised.

'You will drink with me?'

'For good luck . . . to the success of your new venture.'

'But . . .'

'It's true that I have never touched alcohol, but today I will. For you.'

Babu Rao felt like the luckiest man alive. As he began pouring it in a glass, he stopped and asked hesitantly, 'How much?'

'As much as you want me to,' I replied boldly. 'If it is an elixir for you, it is amrit for me too. If it will kill you, I would rather die with you as well. You are the centre around which my whole universe revolves, Rao. I love you.'

He threw his arms around me and, in front of a hundred men and women and waiters and cabaret dancers, kissed me full on the mouth.

The kiss—hard, intense, desperate—wiped the lipstick off my mouth and smeared the make-up I had worn specially for him. Thankfully, the Chanel No. 5 overpowered his stale aftershave.

14

I felt the sharp crack of the whip on my bare flesh. A violently drunk Babu Rao was hulking over me with a whip in his hand. '*Rand*!' he was screaming, over and over again. 'You think you can defy me!' I squirmed out of his grasp and dashed to the door. But as I rattled it, I found it was locked. From behind me, Babu Rao barked again, 'Randi!' He dragged me back by my hair and threw me across the room. My forehead struck the corner of the side table. A hot trickle of blood blurred my eyes. The telephone was ringing, but he did not seem to hear it. Then he leaned down and violently forced my legs apart. He shoved the handle of the whip brutally inside me. I heard another man laughing. I turned to see truck driver Bhajan Lal sitting on the sofa, holding a fiery torch. How could this be? As he flashed the naked flame in my face, I awoke in terror, sweating.

I was in bed. It was morning. The telephone was ringing.

I pieced together fragments from the previous night. We had returned from Blue Nile at 2 a.m. After dropping me, Babu Rao had sped away towards Kamathipura. I had headed straight for the bathroom and had a long shower. I had been holding a tight knot of fear in my stomach all evening and was desperately looking forward to the calming ocean of sleep. But as soon as I hit the bed, I was attacked by an army of thoughts. You are playing with fire, Kumud! Babu Rao is not a fool. One small slip and you will be reduced to a pile of ashes.

The phone continued to ring nonstop. The maid was nowhere to be seen. She had probably gone down to buy freshly baked bread and eggs for breakfast. I rushed to the phone.

'Hello!' I said breathlessly. It was Aabid.

After running around for a few days, he had finally managed to trace Rehmat Khan Lala. That was the previous day, and it was from one of Lala's dens that he had called me up. Unfortunately, we had not been able to talk because of Babu Rao.

We spoke at length now. I had sent, through Aabid, an invitation for Lala to visit the apartment. My plan was to add sleeping pills to the maid's coffee at the time of the meeting.

Rehmat Khan Lala had prudently vetoed my idea. He said meeting in my apartment would be too risky, especially for me: what if Babu Rao walked in unannounced?

Aabid informed me that Lala wanted to fix up the meeting for the following evening at Hotel Shalimar, which was a few blocks down the same street. A private room would be booked so that there would be no chance of us being spotted together. To ensure our safety, we would enter the hotel at separate times and leave separately too. Lala's plan made more sense, I had to accept.

Only one concern remained: what if Babu Rao came to the apartment in my absence? He might smell a rat. His suspicions would be confirmed if he would find the maid sleeping like a log under the influence of pills.

I gave this possibility some thought and hit upon a plan. 'Aabid,' I told him excitedly, 'there is one more task left unfinished.'

'What's it?'

'You need to call Babu Rao . . . today.'

'Is it necessary?'

'I wouldn't have asked if it wasn't.'

'But why?'

'To keep him busy tomorrow night.'

'How?'

'The way you keep me busy for hours.'

He understood. Babu Rao was aware that Aabid was working on a script based on my life. Aabid would call him to fix an appointment for a long interview the following night. But Aabid was still a little sceptical: 'But why will he agree? And to a specific time?'

'Tell him that his character is the hero of your film—the gangster with a heart of gold, who uplifts the whore into a blessed life,' I suggested. In the quicksand of Babu Rao's vanity, any inkling of foul play would sink unnoticed. Aabid agreed it was worth a try.

It struck me that I hadn't revealed my real motive to Aabid. He had no idea what a dangerous game he had got involved in—though he would have guessed by now that my reasons for secretly meeting Lala went beyond financing our film. He was probably imagining that the climax of his story was going to be revealed to me during this clandestine meeting. He would find out how Sattar had met his end. Of course, what he had presumed was not entirely wrong.

The day before the meeting, the sky had been milky-grey since dawn. The sea birds looked unnaturally white against the thunder clouds. The ocean was wild, crashing great operatic overtures against the rocks, each wave stamping as ferociously as a Kathakali dancer. The wet breeze smelled of sea salt. All day, the apartment flickered because of the lightning, as it threatened to rain. But it did not. Just a dull foreboding hung in the air.

The following evening, the sun finally burst through the clouds. I smiled at the maid and declared, 'Today, I am going to make such refreshing coffee that you will remember it your whole life.'

Her face beamed with delight. 'Please don't bother, Ma'am,' she said, the epitome of convent etiquette.

'It's no bother at all.' I smiled. 'You serve me coffee every day. It won't kill me to make coffee for you. Relax . . .'

I went into the kitchen and asked her to sit in the drawing room. I had already crushed the sleeping pills and kept it in my pocket. I pulled out the twist of paper with the powder and added it to one of the cups, stirring it for a few minutes to ensure it dissolved fully. While I did this, I continuously occupied her with questions about her past. She answered enthusiastically, not realizing that I was simply ensuring that she did not have second thoughts about coming to help me.

When I finally walked out into the drawing room with the tray, she was sitting on the sofa like the mistress of the house. I smiled and handed her the special cup, and sat down facing her.

She took the first sip.

'How is it?'

'Oh . . . excellent!' she responded instantly, out of obligation.

I had expected it. I also knew that she would feel duty-bound to keep sipping till she had finished the cup. I emptied mine in one quick gulp and then began leafing idly through the pages of a fashion magazine, glancing sidelong at her from time to time.

After she was done, she thanked me again and got up. Before leaving, she yawned twice—her mouth splitting as wide open as the MGM Studios' lion.

I pretended to yawn and stretched my arms lazily as well. 'I'm going to turn in for the night!' I announced to her as she was leaving.

Ten minutes later, I heard her snoring in her room. I checked the clock. It was half-past nine. Lala was to reach the Hotel Shalimar at ten. I was to make my entry five minutes later. There was still half an hour to go.

I went to the bedroom and picked out my most elegant Punjabi suit—a sober forest green with hand-printed peacock motifs. After I had dressed, I returned to the drawing room and peeped into the maid's room again. Her loud snores, like a car engine repeatedly failing to start, reassured me. She would be out cold at least till the milkman rang the doorbell at dawn.

I hailed a taxi even though Hotel Shalimar was walking distance. I could have gone on foot, but it would seem more appropriate and inconspicuous to drive into a five-star hotel like any other guest.

It was 10.15 p.m. when I reached the lobby of the hotel. I gave the front desk clerk Lala's room number. A porter accompanied me to the elevator and instructed the operator waiting inside. The lift stopped at the third floor and, as I stepped out, the liftman pointed to a room down the long corridor. I started walking towards it.

By then, my stomach was filled with tangled knots that churned with every breath. My heart was beating wildly as I put my finger to the doorbell. A chill gripped my fingers. And then a flood of panic surged down my spine. I felt like running away. What the hell was I doing? Why was I gambling with my life? I could still turn around. Babu Rao would be none the wiser. There was still time . . . I fought off my fear and forced my mind to focus on the reasons for which I had come here. Having come this far, I knew there was no going back.

I could hear the soft sound of the bell ringing inside. Not long after, the door opened. A towering man with a face that seemed like it had been chiselled from rock, and a cropped beard, stood before me. He did not need to introduce himself. He shut the door behind me and led me into the room.

I looked around. On a squat centre table with an inlaid marble top lay an ashtray, on which rested a lighted cigar. A blue curl of smoke floated upwards and mingled with the stationary blades of the ceiling fan.

'Please sit,' said Lala, indicating a sofa.

I sat down. Like a gentleman, he sat facing me. He wore a dark blue Pathani suit, and his hair, which had a few strands of grey, was parted in the middle. He was not yet fifty. Like a typical Kabuli Pathan, he had broad shoulders and a kingly demeanour.

'I am told that you don't drink,' he said with a small smile, picking up the cigar from the ashtray. 'I also don't drink. What shall I order for you?'

'Thums Up will do.'

He pressed a switch on the wall. Moments later, a waiter walked into the room. Lala ordered two bottles and took a long drag of his cigar.

'Tell me,' he said. 'What do you want?'

'Peace of mind.'

He blinked in surprise, but his face remained as calm as a sage.

Before he could say anything, I continued, 'Your peace of mind, too, is linked with it. I have come armed with a foolproof plan to destroy your biggest rival in a single blow.'

'Who is that rival?'

It was my turn to blink in surprise.

'Babu Rao.'

'Oh, that *khatmal*!'

'Yes, him.'

'I have zero interest in that pest. I can swat him down any time he tries to fly too high.'

My heart sank. Of all the things that could have gone wrong, this was not a problem I had foreseen. After everything I had heard from Babu Rao about their fierce rivalry, I never imagined Lala would not even consider Babu Rao worthy of his time. My brain was a tangled nest of thoughts, but I was not going to give up so easily. I had to think of something fast.

'Your rival is not as weak as you think,' I ventured.

'I know him pretty well,' he said confidently. A note of impatience had crept into his voice. As far as he was concerned, the meeting was over.

As he stood up to leave, I played my last card. 'But you don't know that he's aware of all your trade secrets. You are living in a fool's paradise, Lala. Your days are numbered!'

His brows were knitted in annoyance. I knew my audacious claim had bought me only a few seconds more—till he could confirm that he had wasted his evening by meeting an impertinent tart with delusions of grandeur.

'For one,' I said, 'he knows you export headless goats to Dubai only to smuggle drugs.'

Lala stopped. Finally, I had hit the bullseye.

'Are you sure?' he asked gravely, sitting down again.

'Of course. How else would I know this . . . and much more?'

He began to think seriously. He took several thoughtful drags and sat like a mannequin for a very long time. The head of his cigar had begun to ash; it was almost an inch long.

'And you said you have a plan?'

Handing him the ashtray, I said, 'I will share that too. But before that . . .'

I left the sentence unfinished. He understood what I meant.

Rolling the cigar on the ashtray, he tapped the ash out and spoke pragmatically, 'Name your price.'

'If the plan succeeds, you will launch a film production company in my name.'

'And what is the plan?'

'I want to make one point clear before we go any further,' I said, choosing my words carefully. 'I have placed my full trust in you. I will disclose every detail that I know. Maybe you won't agree to go ahead with my plan. Maybe you will. In either case, this meeting must remain a secret. I hope you understand that.'

'I am a Pathan. Betrayal is not in my blood.'

'That's enough. That's all the assurance I need.'

Before I could begin, the waiter came in with a tray bearing two soft drinks. After he laid it down on the table and left, I began disclosing my plan.

The following Tuesday, a ship from Dubai, carrying gold biscuits worth Rs 45 lakh, was to drop anchor three miles off Madh Island. Besides me, there were only a handful of senior cops and customs officials who knew, but Rao had stuffed money in their mouths to silence them.

I continued in a measured tone, 'On Tuesday morning, Babu Rao and his men will take their steam launch straight to the ship. There, in the middle of the sea, wooden crates containing gold are to be transferred to the launch.'

Lala was listening with rapt attention, his body as motionless as his eyes. This pleased me. Between his fingers, the cigar with its red mouth was going up in smoke, just like Babu Rao's future.

After I finished, Lala seemed lost in his thoughts for a while. The cigar had nearly gone out. Before it could singe his fingers, he dropped it into the ashtray and poured a few drops of his drink over the sizzling stub to cool it.

'Do you know the code word?' he asked.

I nodded.

He extended his hand. I shook it.

The deal was sealed.

'Kumud,' he said, using my name for the first time, 'even if the plan fails, I will launch a production house in your name. I value those who wish me well. What is the code?'

'The tandel of the Dubai ship will ask, "How many roses did you lay on grandma's grave?"'

'What's the answer?'

'Ten roses.'

Our conversation lasted an entire hour. Though we were sitting behind the closed doors of a hotel room, he did not once attempt to touch me. His gaze did not have any trace of lust. I was impressed.

As I got up to leave, he accompanied me to the door and even opened it for me.

As he walked with me to the lift, I asked, 'Can I ask you a question?'

'Sure.'

'There was a boy named Sattar who used to work in your liquor den in Kamathipura . . .'

I did not need to say more.

'I wish you had not asked.' His face became grim.

'Why not?'

'What do you want to know?'

'Is he alive?'

'No.'

My feet seemed stuck to the ground. I felt as if I was rooted to the spot. Eventually, he gave me a brief account of what had happened. Sattar had come to meet me at the air-conditioned bungalow. He was drunk. The bouncer did not allow him to proceed upstairs. Upset, Sattar began to hurl abuses at him. The bouncer responded by giving him a resounding slap. A fuming Sattar attacked him, unaware that he was not alone. Two more goondas, who were close by, appeared on the scene. Together, the three of them reduced Sattar to a pulp. They twisted his elbows backward till they snapped. Then they cut off his penis with a Rampuri and tossed it to a stray dog. If that was not enough, they poured acid over his face, disfiguring it completely. He lost both eyes in that barbaric attack.

To send out a strong message, Sattar was carried in that horrific state to Lala's liquor joint by Babu Rao's men and dumped inside. His screams had been heartrending. He was not asking for vengeance, but for death. His screams were so loud that Lala came to the spot.

Lala could not bear the sight of Sattar screeching his heart out. Death was better than a life without a face, eyes, arms, legs or a penis. Lala took a decision on the spot. He aimed his revolver at Sattar's head and ended his misery.

I shuddered.

Had Lala done Sattar a favour? From a moralistic perspective, it would seem wrong for Lala to take Sattar's life. He should not have played God. But from a human angle, I felt Lala was right. If I had been in his place, under those circumstances, I would probably have—

Actually, I don't know what I would have done. But there was no need for an answer. Sattar was no longer in this world. For the first time in my life, I felt the vastness of the emptiness within myself. He was gone. I could not sleep that night. All my life I had been a fighter—every challenge, every defeat, every abuse had made me only stronger and more determined—but that night all the fight left me. Sadness wrestled me to the ground: I was no match for it. I cried soft tears as I remembered the bright-eyed boy who would give me running commentary with a double omelette and a cup of chai. The man who taught me there was something clean and pure and loving inside of me—something that was only my own—that no man could ever defile. The lover whose body always had the secret remedy to the aching loneliness of my life. Suddenly, this loneliness hit me with full force. I could taste salt in my throat: the curtains had come down on the first and last love of my life. I had never imagined it would have such a tragic end.

For a moment, my mind jumped to Aabid who was looking for a suitable ending for his script. He would certainly be charged up hearing how Sattar's death had played out. He would find the climax he had been looking for. The first act of my life would also end here.

Lala called me up the following week. Dawood had successfully intercepted the ship carrying gold biscuits. A few hours before intercepting the ship, he had set Babu Rao's boat, which was still tied to the shore, on fire. Before Babu Rao could make alternative arrangements, Dawood had reached the ship mid-sea and claimed all the gold.

Lala advised me to leave Babu Rao's apartment as soon as possible because I knew his secret. A compromised police or customs official could have leaked the news of the gold crossing, but I was the only one who knew the code. It would take Babu Rao just a few minutes to join the dots. If he found me in the apartment, I would be as good as dead.

'Lala, I want to go back to my village for a few days.'

'It's a good idea to leave town. I will send someone to book the tickets. You pack your bags. I'll personally come to pick you up in the next thirty minutes.'

The maid was busy in the kitchen. I explained the matter to her as innocently as possible. 'My mother is serious. I have to leave for the village as soon as possible.'

This was not entirely untrue. A few days earlier, when I had received Aai's letter informing me about her terminal illness, I had read out the relevant portion to her. She probably assumed that I had received an urgent telegram from the village. Leaving aside all her work in the kitchen, she threw herself into packing my suitcase. Meanwhile, I changed into a plain, dark salwar-kameez for the train journey.

Before Lala arrived, I did receive a telegram. Aai had passed away a week before. The last link to my past was gone. I stood in the doorway, my head reeling. I was about to collapse when Lala, who had just come out of the elevator, rushed to my side to support me.

'What happened?' he asked, astonished.

I rested my head on his shoulder and broke down.

The maid appeared nervously a little distance away at the door, her face furrowed with lines of confusion and fear.

Before she could make sense of the scene, Lala had picked up my suitcase. I followed him into the lift. While going down, I informed him about my mother's death. I didn't know where to go now. It made no sense to go back to the village any more.

'Kumud, you don't worry. For the time being, you move into my vacant apartment at Marine Drive. After that, it's entirely up to you.'

Before the elevator reached the ground floor, we heard gunshots. Lala became alert. 'The khatmal is here.' He referred to Babu Rao only by that name. He pulled out a gun and kept it poised in his hand, finger on the trigger.

Through the small glass pane in the elevator door, I saw Lala's Mercedes parked in front of the entrance. Lala's men had taken position behind it. Their backs were to us. Babu Rao's car was across the road, next to the pavement. Two of his men had taken cover behind a Gulmohar tree.

Both gangs had positioned themselves strategically. Between them flowed a stream of rush-hour traffic, packed with vehicles headed back home to the suburbs.

Another shot rang out. The bullet had found its mark: one of Babu Rao's men let out a cry and collapsed on the pavement across the road. In response, Babu Rao's men fired three shots targeting Lala's Mercedes. One of the bullets pierced the windshield, leaving a pin-sized hole and a cobweb of cracks.

We had come out of the lift but were still in the passage of the ground floor, where it was safe. It would be foolish to step out of the building amidst the firing. I glanced at Lala. He seemed to be thinking fast.

Suddenly, he pulled my wrist and dashed towards the lift. We returned to my apartment and went to the balcony, which overlooked the street. The maid was already there, taking in all the action. When she saw Lala, she began screeching and babbling in fear.

Lala grabbed her by the scruff of the neck and shook her vigorously. She crumpled in a heap on the floor. Lala then positioned himself behind a large flowerpot. I stood next to him.

The balcony offered a clear view. From this height, we could see Babu Rao and his remaining men scampering across the road like rats. I watched hypnotized. It was just a matter of a few minutes. The man I loathed would be struck from the face of the earth.

The sound of gunshots had also aroused the curiosity of the neighbours. Soon, there were nervous faces at the windows. A few residents had gathered cautiously in their balconies. Traffic had come to a standstill. One of the bullets had hit the driver of a passing car that had overturned in the middle of the road. A long queue of vehicles with horns blaring incessantly had formed behind it.

Lala took careful aim from the balcony. After leaving the weapon, the bullet found its way into Babu Rao's skull and exploded. Fragments of his head splattered around, leaving a fountain of gushing blood behind. Before my very eyes, the man who had raped me and celebrated the killing of my lover fell to the ground, dead.

It would have been suicidal for Babu Rao's men to carry on without their commander. They knew they had lost—all that remained of their boss was a headless body. Lala's men had stopped firing as well. Nobody wanted any more bloodshed.

I accompanied Lala to the ground floor again. Both sides had suffered casualties. Babu Rao was dead, as were two of his associates. One more was grievously injured. The two men, who were fortunate to be alive, fled with the injured gang members.

Lala, too, had lost two men. One had been shot in the head and the other in the chest. The third one was alive but critical. Lala helped the fourth one, the sole survivor, place the bodies into the boot of the car. The injured man was propped upright in the back seat. Lala and I sat in the front and sped to Kamathipura.

I realized that a massive storm had passed through my life, leaving me unscathed. But after every storm comes a calm. Slowly, one's life begins to settle down into new routines, a new normality returns. With the passage of time, my life, too, came back on track.

Rehmat Khan Lala allowed me to stay in his Marine Drive flat for as long as I wanted. He also kept his word and launched a production house for me. I put Aabid in charge of it. He enthusiastically started doing all the groundwork for the film. He hired a team to take care of production and brought a fresh director on board. I was to be the lead actress. This is what I had dreamt of.

I cannot say whether the film will be a success or a flop. I do not care either. It is enough that in this little lifetime so many things I desired came my way one after the other. I moved from the pavement to the cages, from the cages to Gangu Bai's brothel, from there to an air-conditioned villa, and then to a penthouse in a posh neighbourhood.

Today, I am an actress. If my film turns out to be a flop, I can always become the mistress of some wealthy man, or even marry a rich industrialist, though I have not given marriage much thought. Lala did express interest in marrying me, but I wasn't ready for it. Why, you ask? Because his religion lawfully allows him four wives and he already has four. That means I can marry him only if he gives talaq to one of them—and that is something I don't want. However, I would not mind becoming his mistress.

That would be marvellous.